PHARMACOLOGY

PHARMACOLOGY

A NOVEL BY
CHRISTOPHER HERZ

PUBLISHED BY

Text copyright ©2011 Christopher Herz
All rights reserved
Printed in the United States of America

Published by AmazonEncore
P.O. Box 400818
Las Vegas, NV 89140

ISBN-13: 9781612181387
ISBN-10: 1612181384

For Mom—
You always knew I'd get here.

CHAPTER 1

i.

Everyone wants more stories about the junkie-vampire-strip-per-sex-dungeon-bloodletting-in-front-of-sushi-eating-Hell's-Angels-and-My-Little-Pony-collecting folks I lived with in San Francisco inside that old Victorian on McAllister that used to be a brothel in the twenties.

You can find out more about them in *Luddite #3: The Roommates Issue*. *Luddite* was a zine we published from 1993 through '95 in an attempt to hold on to the world before it switched over.

Lived in that house about a year. Moved in six months after I'd landed in the city. Left after they started stealing my socks. Junkies usually don't do their own laundry. Can still hear Mom telling me in that Kansas City (that's Kansas City, Missouri, not Kansas) accent she never lost:

"Sarah Striker, you best make sure you have on those clean socks," she'd say without looking up. "Keeping feet warm and bad things away are important when you're digging around at that Salvation Army."

She knew there was no sense in dragging me to church on Sundays, so she took the day for herself and God and let my pops and me do what we loved.

We'd cruise the old Impala down East Truman Road to the best Salvation Army in town. The outside of his ride was beat-up as hell, but the insides ran just perfect—perfect enough for our Sunday drives, anyhow.

The Salvation Army down there had a twenty-five-cent book section filled with all the stuff that nobody else wanted. Stocked up on these old trashy novels and super spy stories that weren't all that super—didn't much care what the book was about—it was more about gathering quantity. Turn them into something.

My pops was always looking for a project—some old radio or fan or turntable he could fix up and get working again. We'd meet up at the register with our stashes and drive back with giant smiles on our faces.

Now Moms didn't like eating out all that much—felt it was just too dirty to be served by someone else—so when we had the chance, Pops and I would go on down to Chubby's, eat a righteous burger and some onion rings, clean up, and get home just about the time she was coming home from church.

"I need to rest a bit," she'd say before crashing out on the couch and drinking herself a little bit of the Hennessey that I'd drink a little bit more of once she went to sleep.

Spent time in my room playing records, cutting out little sentences from each of the books, and pasting them on whatever paper I could find until I had a story formed. My mind always arranged images and words as it saw fit. Figured that if what I wanted to read didn't exist, might as well do it myself. When I had my story, I'd create a little book out of regular paper that I could carry around in my back pocket. Didn't do any copying back then, so each book I created was unique. Had no idea what I was doing was called a zine—just felt good creating my own reality and have it exist as something I could touch. Invited some of my friends over to listen to records with me at first and help with the cutting and pasting, but they were all listening to Poison and Warrant back then, so I sat alone with my Public Enemy record—the first one when it was all mono recorded. They just kind of looked at each other with contorted faces and made up excuses why they had to leave.

> *Suckas to the left, I know you hate my 98! You*
> *gonna get yours!*
>
> *—Public Enemy*

Be a little lit while doing my book mash-ups from the sips I took of Mom's drink, but it made things warmer when there wasn't enough heat.

We rented our garage out to the neighbors who needed extra storage, so Pops had his projects set up on this little TV folding table that sat right next to the kitchen table.

Made sure I had it all set up when he came home at around one a.m. He took up a second job developing photographs for this shop on the other side of town. Man who owned the shop paid cash, so it was clear money we used on groceries and fun stuff like the Salvation Army.

Mom would be passed out already because she had to be up at five a.m. to get ready for her route. Drove all the kids to school, and had been doing it for so long that nobody minded much if she was late for picking up a kid now and then.

Be a little drunk and he'd be a lot tired, so eating a meal at one a.m. made good sense for both of us.

Usually cooked up a grilled cheese.

"You thinking about school?" he asked one night. "Your mom should be keeping your mind on school. It doesn't have to be around here, either."

"Won't be around here," I told him, taking the sandwich out of the pan and onto a plate. "Picked a solid place, though. I'll work a decent gig at night, so my being away won't be a cash strain. You built me so I can stand on my own. No more second shifts, Pop."

"Where's it at?" he said, looking at me proudly, like he would at some antique record player he'd just brought back to life.

"San Francisco," I told him, placing his plate in front of him. "San Francisco State University. About four hundred a semester. Sounds doable, no?"

"They have a football team I can follow from here?" he asked, looking to make sure I cooked his grilled cheese just right. "The Chiefs aren't much of anything this year, and I could use someone to root for."

"Just root for me, Pops. I'll take care of the championship."

He smiled, but it dropped a little bit. Usually would catch him in moments of tiredness and searching for strength, but this was something different—like he had something to say but wanted to find a moment that wouldn't stick solid in my memory.

"There's not an easy way to say any of this," he said, touching the corner of the sandy and then licking the tip of his finger. "I've been having some problems and hoping they'd go away, but it's just not happening."

"Most of the expenses will get covered with a job, Pops, so don't worry too much."

"No—it's not money problems, Sarah," he said, wiping his mouth and taking a breath. "It's cancer. I've been trying to get treated, but the doctor told me this afternoon that there's nothing out there on the market to take care of this. We're going to have to go with some experimental procedures."

Now this was the same doctor that Moms made him see a few years back when she thought he was so down all the time, but really he was just tired of looking back on what he could have done with his life. Pretty sure most people get lost for bits like that. During her drives to work, she'd hear these spots on the radio talking about depression—talking about the *symptoms* of depression.

If you think you've been experiencing depression, or someone you love is acting listless, has low energy, seems withdrawn, and is not able to do the things they normally do, ask your doctor about what medication may be right for you or your family. Depression is a real condition that may lead to serious illnesses if not treated.

What nobody paid too much attention to at the time, especially my mom, were items called adverse events that came on afterwards at breakneck speed. Later they'd make laws to correct that.

May cause drowsiness, loss of vision, and cancer in some men over the age of forty.

Moms didn't like seeing the man she married slogging around the house, tired from a job he never wanted to do. It wasn't the future she felt she deserved. Guess that's tough being trapped in something like that.

We both looked at each other without saying a word. Knew my pops very well. He'd taken that job with the DMV and figured that even though it would be rough, his insurance was going to cover everything for the family. After all, that's why he took the damn gig in the first place: so he could have some stability in case anything happened to me along the way to turning eighteen.

Before he had me, he photographed garage bands in Kansas City and would hold shows where folks would turn out on weekend nights to look at pictures of what was taking place in the underground. Some would even buy the prints, which, he told me over a few of our kitchen table sessions, would be the highlight of the day. He was thinking of making a career of it and even started sending them out to big magazines to see if he could land a job or an assignment, but before he ever heard anything back, he had gotten my mom pregnant, and that was it for his dreams of going off into the world of rock 'n' roll.

"Why didn't you just keep going with the photography?" I asked him once. "In the long run, you wouldn't have made a grip doing what you loved."

"The long run wasn't in my sights," he said.

Never asked him about it again.

He took that job at the DMV not too long after finding out about me. Made sure he was the one taking the pictures of those sixteen-year-olds about to get behind the wheel.

Pops gave up so much for me to get out of Kansas City, so the words saying *Don't go* wouldn't spill from his lips. Knew that he wasn't going to be able to work anymore, and there was no way Mom's bus driving was going to pay for what we needed.

"They say that since they can't know if I got the cancer from my job or from the depression medication, they won't pay for the treatment. And even if they would, none of the doctors in my plan can do what I need done. So, the woman I spoke with today from the insurance company, well, she called back from a different number. Told me of some new studies they were doing at the university. I go in Monday."

He took another bite and kept his eyes on me but couldn't find his smile. A minute of silenced passed in agony as the clicks from the second hand of the clock on the wall moved, though it might have also been the mouse we could never catch moving in the walls.

"I'm still going to San Francisco," I told him, taking a bite of my own. "Only, I don't need to go to school. Can learn whatever art I need from the city itself. Work should be much easier to find there, and I'll send cash home so we can get you some proper treatment."

"Mom's not going to let you forget about school."

"Almost an adult, so don't need permission. Besides, it's the better financial decision. There's more work out there than in Kansas City. Besides, everyone knows you go out west if you want to find gold!"

We sat together with the sounds of biting perfectly buttered bread and melted cheese providing our soundtrack. That table was my base. In the years that followed, when times turned to madness, I always placed myself there with my pops. He was well. We were all well. Just needed to put the pieces together like I always did.

2.

Issue #1 of *Luddite* had pictures backstage of the O'Farrell Theater where one of my roommates danced. She was a fantastic writer and a good earner too. Made nearly five hundred cash a night doing whatever she did onstage and backstage, but spent just as much on what she put up her arm once she got home. Well, that's not right. She shot behind her knees and other parts so the stuff people paid to see stayed clean.

Her live-in boyfriend wasn't as motivated, but he did wear silver Underoos around the house while waiting for her to come home.

Like her, he had porcelain fangs surgically inserted into his gums. He was tall, pale, and very skinny. He grew up in Hawaii, so guess he had to hate the sun and all of those tan people making fun of him. Doll dresses with holes cut out of them hung on a wall next to the antique glass cabinet guarding every My Little Pony ever made. When you talked to him, he'd do their hair with a special little sterling comb he'd carved his initials into and wore on a chain around his neck.

Back then, you'd go shopping for rooms to move into and live in a place with a bunch of folks who had been there long before you and pay them around three hundred dollars a month.

When I called back home to check in with my pops, I'd keep all the adventure and vampires in the stories, but I'd leave out the drugs because he'd get worried and I couldn't have that.

Landed a job at a café right away.

There were about seven people in total living in the house, but only two were vampires. The others were a skater-punk-whore guy who looked like a goat and always picked his skin when he was high, but who had a good heart and let you smoke his cigarettes, so he was okay by me because they were KOOLs, which I enjoyed every now and then. He shared his room with a rather large girl who had, like many girls in San Francisco, lost herself in the madness of the city and was drowning herself in junk thinking it was love.

The other two spots were always rotating around and, for some reason, were always a couple.

Now, when I first moved in, and even after a few months of family meetings, I had no idea they were junkies. Had never seen heroin other than in the movies. Most my friends could afford back in Kansas City was some low-level speed that I was never really much into. Looked like crushed orange Nerds. Burroughs lived around where I grew up, but he had already made it and could afford his habit.

After we agreed on everything and I moved my things in, Valerie, the female vamp, told me that she and Darren D. (her man) would be performing that night at the Trucedero and they'd put me on the list.

Went downstairs and across the street to look at what was about to be my new home.

The outside of the building was purple with golden trim. There was this hard clamshell awning hanging over the top of the stoop. Three apartments actually in there, but ours was the top. You could see two giant oval windows looking over the top like eyes that had lost their lids. There were two levels to the one we lived in. The skater-punk goat-face boy and his heavy girl-friend lived on the first floor, and next to them was the room that people were always moving out of. A staircase sprang from the living room to the next floor, which is where my room and the vampires' were. Was just off to the side of the old fifty-foot ballroom with giant windows that looked over the city. The view was incredible. A long hallway led down to the vampires' room, which was far enough away from me that pretty much made the entire ballroom mine. In the middle of the hallway, a deck looked out over the rooftops.

Called up my pops, but my mom said he had just gone to sleep, as the medicine was making him sleepy. She put the phone up to his ear and let me tell him about my new place. Pretty sure it got into his ears.

Half asleep, I could hear him say through his dreams, "I never had a doubt."

3.

"Enjoy," the man holding the ropes and struggling to stay within his T-shirt said. "You got good people looking out for you, honey—getting on the list tonight was nearly impossible. I used to have that." His kind voice didn't match the rattling chain connecting his nose ring to his ear.

Inside, the music was pretty heavy house, I guess, though I can't be sure. Never knew the difference between techno and house, but I didn't much like either of them. First time I heard Public Enemy, I couldn't hear anything else.

Couldn't gauge how big the place was because the low lighting mixed with black walls took away my depth perception. No doubt that if you had turned the lights on, it would have been just another room, but the absence of illumination is sometimes the best way to start an adventure.

Took a deep breath and moved on through the thick air that mixed with sweat, alcohol, and anticipation. Everyone was looking around to see when something would start happening. The only light came from the bar against the wall and a spotlight that lit up what was trying to pull itself off as a stage.

There were a few men in black polo shirts walking around with clipboards trying to get people's phone numbers. They looked totally out of place. One of them approached me but thought better of asking me any questions when he saw my eyes burning through him. Never liked to be asked anything by strangers.

The guy vampire saw me and came up with a fistful of drink tickets and a big smile.

"It's me! Darren D.! You came!" he said. "Oh my God! That's awesome. We were wondering, 'Is she going to show?' Do you need something to drink? We can drink whatever—for *free*."

Tons of Hell's Angels there, or at least they were dressed like Hell's Angels. You couldn't tell. May have been stockbrokers during the day.

All eating sushi.

"Valerie's about to go on," he said, grabbing my hand and leading me through the crowd of maybe-Hell's-Angels sushi face-stuffers. His Hello Kitty bracelet bounced against my wrist.

Valerie was onstage dressed in a long leather robe and holding a whip. The stagehand was just finishing tying up this bald-headed girl with a tattoo on the top of her head and large hoops stretching out her lobes. My new roommate was measuring her row of perfectly aligned syringe needles neatly laid on a table. Valerie saw me and waved hello with a huge smile.

"Cool," Darren D. said, sipping quickly on his drink while waving at the cocktail waitress to bring over another. "You're good, right? Nice! It's about to start. It's amazing. She's amazing."

Darren D. moved next to the tied-up girl, nodded at Valerie, and then, with the same look as my old doctor in Kansas City used to have, started sticking needles into the back of her knees to draw out blood from the baldheaded girl before feeding it back to her.

Valerie moved five measured steps back and started cracking her whip.

The sushi-eating Hell's Angels cheered and clapped. The baldheaded girl had an even expression on her face. Out of the corner of my eye, I saw one of the black polo shirt guys snap a picture of the girl being fed blood.

Turned to one of the Hell's Angels and said, "Those are my new roommates."

Everyone was having a fantastic time.

4.

Show ended at five a.m.

Mornings in San Francisco are always cold no matter what time of year it is. The heavy fog had soaked into my skin from the night before, so instead of going to sleep, I stood outside of Kinko's and waited until the sun came to help evaporate the moisture.

Went in and got to work while everything was still fresh in my head. Everything I needed was right there: Sharpie, stapler, paper, glue, copying machine, and tons of light. *Luddite #2: The Dominance Issue*. Made a Hell's Angels logo by photocopying a patch this guy who couldn't stop looking at me ripped off his jacket and wrote his phone number on. Cut that out and glued it on the page that was to become the cover, then surrounded that logo with a whip I drew. Was going to put the vamps on there, but Ann Rice at that point in history was dominating the scene and I didn't want Tom Cruise's face coming into my vision.

My resources were limited, so I had to use words to put it all down in ink—the sushi, the faces, the Hello Kitty. Documentation. Had to press hard as hell to make sure it came out legible in the copies. Best thing about Kinko's so late at night is that they didn't empty the trash, so if I had to have images, I would just look through what people threw away and use those—it was random but sincere, which is all I cared about.

There was always company at Kinko's—either homeless people stepping in from the streets or fanatics making flyers to pass out. On this night, there was a kid struggling to get what he wanted out of his flyer—must have been fifteen drafts crumpled on the table beside him. Not so much a kid, actually, but age was never something I could really figure out. The top of his flyer read:

The Lobbyists Are Coming!

He was trying to draw a bike messenger riding across the top of the page like Paul Revere holding up a bottle of pills, but he wasn't getting the results he wanted. The attempts at drawings were kind of cute. Took one of them off of his trash pile, cut out the bike part, and glued it on the bottom of one of the pages.

"You're not going to even read it?" he asked, handing me the draft he was most proud of. "Might change the way you look at the world."

Folded it up and put it in the back pocket of my Levi's.

"That's happened enough to me," I said, holding up my newly stapled copy of *Luddite*.

He smiled, but not at me, more like he was laughing at me from the future, looking back at the moment. He finished his printing and put the stack of flyers into his messenger bag. Noticed two of his knuckles had recently been scraped.

"Trade you," I said, handing him a copy. "You better read the whole thing."

"Same here," he said, pointing at the flyer in my pocket and smiling.

Checked my watch. Playtime was over. Liked to get to the café so I'd be the one opening. That way I could call home and rap with my pops a little bit while I was having my breakfast. We never talked about whatever treatments he was going through. He never brought them up, and I never wanted to hear. Figured sending him the cash and telling him about the madness of San Francisco was enough.

A group of skater boys would come by while I was opening the café and show off, doing tricks around me. It was the end of the OJ 2 Hard Riders wheels. They were just about to change over to those skinny ones I never understood. They would trade me mix tapes for cookies and coffees, which was outstanding. It's how I found out about the Gravediggaz, Del, and Souls of Mischief. Even at that point, nobody was playing much of that on the radio. You needed to hear it from someone else.

"Positive Energy Activates Constant Elevation."

—The RZA

Worked up in Bernal Heights, just above the Mission District. It was a small, professional lesbian community. The café served high-class organic food and was run by two gearhead brothers who made tons of money and wore cool motorcycle boots. They both wanted to be punk rock stars but got rich in real estate, so they bought the spot to feel some ties to a bohemian lifestyle.

Was reading *Street Players* then by Donald Goines and loving each word of it.

Man, that guy could write.

The two brothers—who looked the same, but not really—would come in at different times and take money from the drawer for a girl or some coke or whatever it is they wanted to buy. That worked for me because they always needed weed, so I usually stopped by Dolores Park before I went to work and bought some off of the cholos who had it buried under the grass.

Families were playing with their kids or dogs or whatever around us.

Sell it back to the two brothers at a double markup, so it worked out well. Sometimes being in the middle is enough to survive if you know how to do it.

Because they were so into music, the CDs in the shop were good to listen to while making coffee and serving up sandwiches. They had a bunch of Leonard Cohen, the Animals, the Clash, Velvet Underground—pretty much a bunch of stuff that was never on my turntable at home but now was in my ears.

Something about the Animals that stayed with me and made the working time there go right. Couldn't listen to them anywhere but there.

The city seemed so far away, and the café up here, the reason I liked it so much was because it felt like secret lives were being lived inside the houses that stood guard in the neighborhood, each one trying to be more different than the others.

5.

My schedule was so different from my new roommates'. They worked at night mostly. Valerie stripped (she called it dancing), and Darren D., well, he didn't really work at all, except for the sidekick duties of scoring heroin and assisting her in daytime gigs. There was tons of work for them, especially during the lunch hours.

Darren D. and Valerie rented an apartment in the Tenderloin that they turned into a sex dungeon and waited for clients to come in during their lunch break from whatever office they were working at. Some would come in and get tied up in a chair and be interrogated like they were Nazi war criminals. Or be the janitor who got beaten for not cleaning up the mess. Whatever they wanted to be punished as, they were punished for.

They had this huge dog that looked like a mad wolf, and sometimes they'd tie up a businessman and question him with "Tactics." Think they had some type of group sex at the end of it all—in some way. Sex doesn't always mean intercourse, which was one of the things I found out when I left Kansas City and came to San Francisco.

Then, after everything was done, the guy or girl would pay, put on their clothes after a nice shower, and return to the office good and relaxed.

Everyone worked.

Even the skater goat-faced boy worked. His name was Kurt, but I never knew his last name. He wasn't into the cruel stuff. Wasn't his thing. Like, the vamps got paid to break into this rich couple's house (paid by the couple they were attacking) in Pacific Heights once a month and brutally attack them at random times.

Kurt would do things like sit with an older man who was even older than his age because he was dying of AIDS and strip down to his underwear and watch documentaries about bees making honey. There was no touching involved at all. Got paid three hundred cash for those sessions. The best part about that, for me at least, was that the guy dying of AIDS got all of this medical marijuana that he gave to Kurt, who didn't like to smoke because it did nothing for him, so he'd give it to me. Turned that around by selling it to the two brothers who owned the café. All of that went directly home to Pops and allowed me to live my life a little better in the city because I knew I was generating cash and sending it home.

CHAPTER 2

i.

Still have the smell of markers and spray paint in my nostrils.

Two of my good friends, Colin Chapman and Nicholas Mot, were art school dropouts who took solace in their underground graffiti fame. Colin was a true master with the can. Remember just watching him for hours at a time while he kept going from his book of sketches to the wall, making sure his vision made it onto the bricks and concrete.

Nick was more interested in his name getting up everywhere in the city so he'd be known. Nothing against that, either—there was an art to gaining recognition.

They had a very small place up in Pacific Heights—a bunk bed I think was pretty much all that fit in the room. A bunch of yuppies and flower shops around them. The apartment, or studio—I guess it was a studio—was covered in markers and Krylon. Colin was usually practicing body poses in some book, where he'd draw different versions of himself as a superhero cartoon character. Words took form in thought bubbles filled with hip-hop lines from songs that were going to be classics at one point, but at that time were just what we all listened to.

> *You couldn't come to the jungles of the East poppin' that game*

*You won't survive get live catchin' wreck is our
thing
I don't gang bang or shoot out bang bang
The relentless lyrics the only dope I slang*

—Jeru the Damaga

That was the first comic that I'd publish in *Luddite*. Colin took the all of the lyrics from Jeru the Damaga's "Come Clean" and split them up into dialogue. Amazing.

Carried his black book everywhere and handled it so soft— like cradling a child.

At this point, there still wasn't that much light on the hip-hop world. It was right before Biggie and everything that came after him.

It was the summer after Black Sheep, just before the first Wu was to come out. Nas was on his way. The Pharcyde tape played in all of our yellow Sony Walkmen, where you had to hold the bottom piece down so that the music would play out of both sides of the headphones.

Colin would go off by himself at times and just be in his head with whatever he was drawing. Learned that from early childhood of sometimes no roof, ninety-nine-cent store food, blankets made of jackets that weren't enough to cover him and his sister, and hands that caused bruises that spread beneath the skin. He would smile great, but as soon as it faded, there was a terrible sadness on his face.

When he went out at night, we went with him. Didn't really much like writing on walls or trucks, though shoe polish on bus stops in the Fillmore was kind of fun. Late at night the city slowed down, the tourists ducked into their hotels, and the true life started.

2.

Down on Lower Haight all the graph writers would hang out at the Horseshoe Café. That bathroom was legendary because of the hieroglyphics left with every type of writing tool you could imagine. People talk bullshit all day long. Ben Davis shirts, Fresh Jive Pants, and Pumas with Phat laces, which were throwbacks even then.

Never slept in late, even if we had been out late the night before.

Colin and Nick were hanging outside the Horseshoe when I came up on them. They were anything but daytime people. Nick was an enigma to me. Lost in clouds of smoke and restless inside of his own body when the sun was out or there wasn't anyone looking at him. He was always on the go and asking you to go with him, but whenever you got somewhere with him, he'd make sure there was enough space between the two of you so he'd stand out.

"What's up with your roommates?" he asked. "I heard they drink blood."

"No, they don't drink it," I told him. "They take it out of other people and feed it back to them."

He played out the vision in his head and laughed. "I wouldn't mind checking that out. I'm good with crazy people. Anything for a good show, you know?"

"Just come through whenever the sun's down—they get off work late."

"I'm too busy to come through. There's tons to do."

Colin looked up a second from his sketching and commented to himself, then pulled his ball cap down low and continued with what he was doing. "We got to get to the Cliff House before the sun gets down," he said, packing up his book before anyone could say something.

He walked up to the bus stop just as the 71 pulled up. We waited for the back doors to open and walked in among the stream of people walking out.

3.

Gifted Unlimited Rhymes Universal.

Guru's *Jazzmatazz* played over and over again. Everyone was listening. Even the old Beats who sat across the street from City Lights at Café Trieste thinking about how the days have moved past them and they were never included in the same category of the glorious three. Or glorious four—however you want to look at it.

Through the scratched-over windows of the bus, the old Victorians passed by us, large-scale dollhouses that required the souls of those who built the city to stay in the carved-out wood and perfectly painted exteriors.

We got off the bus and reached the edge of the city, with only the Great Highway separating us from where the Cliff House stood glorious against the Pacific. Inside was a restaurant serving decent Irish coffee and good food, but we weren't there for that. We came for the arcade.

The Musée Mécanique was an old-style arcade with machines from the twenties and thirties that used to take a nickel or a penny and allow for escape from your world. You'd glance down and look at an old flip-book or see what passed as pornography sixty years ago. My favorites were the old baseball card machines that only cost a quarter to get a replica of an old Jackie Robinson card.

There were glass-enclosed opium dens, vampires that came out of coffins, and carnivals that sprang into action when you dropped in a coin. Kept smelling the ocean crashing around the cliffs the whole place was built on, so I stepped outside and gave my pops a call and shared the moment with him.

Dialed up from the payphone and waited for his voice to join the breeze.

"Hey, Pops, how you feeling?"

"Better now that you're on the other end. Where you calling me from today?"

"Looking out over the Pacific, Pops," I told him, trying to let him hear the waves, the seals on the rock just in front of me, and my voice all at the same time. "Wanted to share this with you. Something other than the money, you know?"

"My baby girl," he said, trying not to let me hear his cough. "The money is helping more than you know. Even the little bit of it. You're doing all of this from a café?"

"You need more, Pops?"

There was a quick silence before the voices switched and my mother came on the line.

"Sarah—your father got a little too excited. You hear what it's doing to him in the background, no?"

He started in pretty good again.

"Mom—tell me the truth. Is the money I'm sending home helping at all?"

I heard her walk out of his earshot.

"Sarah—the money you are sending is helping, but the bills are getting to be too much. There's only so many extra shifts I can take. The trials they are running now are helping, but the side effects from the drugs are causing other problems and the insurance company won't cover these because they say they won't cover experimental procedures. Can you ask your boss for a raise?"

I didn't know what to say, but I knew that I couldn't ask for any raise. Those guys were putting money up their nose. I'd have to make a switch.

"No problem, Moms. I'll take care of it. Give him a kiss for me and let him know there's magic inside of it."

My time ran out before I could ask anything about her and how she was dealing with everything.

Colin rolled out with his book sketching an old baseball game played with a metal ball and a bat activated by pinball flippers. Each of the men on the field were reciting different Wu Tang lyrics.

CHAPTER 3

i.

Handle Remi was one of those strange guys in the city who could sleep with anybody he happened to feel attracted to that day because he sold everything that kept the city awake. Wasn't into him or what he was about, but he had a big crush on Colin and let him post up and draw whatever he wanted while girls and boys of all types made their way through his den.

Handle lived just up the hill that led down to the Castro. His apartment was unassuming from the outside, one of the more normal places in the city, but inside, in that living room and behind the closed doors of the bedroom, the deeper you looked, the more intense it got. There were girls everywhere, but they made sure not to pay attention to anyone more than they did Handle. He was so flamboyant and clean. Think he got up in the middle of conversations to go into the bathroom and shave his arms.

Met this girl Jenny over there. Colin and Nick were back on the couch zooted out of their heads, but my eyes were on her. She wore these gray stretch pants that were tight around her entire body and a V-neck T-shirt that outlined her breasts in such a way that they seemed perfectly round whichever way she moved.

She was so comfortable and confident in her body. Myself, I slouched sometimes so I wouldn't carry my full height. Was tall for every age I ever was. My pops wanted me to go out for the basketball team, but my breasts came in kind of early, so it wasn't much fun to jump all the time with those things flopping everywhere. Jenny was a few years older than me, already eyeing college and looking to get into the other world. I saw her checking me out.

Every time I met someone with the name Jennifer I always thought of that De La Soul song.

"Want to grab something to eat?" I asked.

"Don't you think you should, like, ask me my name?" she said, pulling back and lifting up the V in her shirt.

"I know your name," I told her. "Jenny, right? We've talked before."

"Well, I don't know yours, but I'm hungry. Come on, we'll grab a cab."

Needed to clear my head to figure out my next move. Pops needed money, and I needed to stay out here to make it. No way I was going back.

Jenny was light and beautiful, and I jumped with her. Figured I could get my mind off of things and then the next solution would come to me.

She got her stuff together, and I nodded at the boys on the couch. Couldn't be afraid to make a break from people—there was too much to accomplish.

Jenny put her hoodie on, kissed Handle on the cheek, then led me downstairs and out to the streets to inject into the vein of the city again. She hailed a cab, and we jumped in. Thinking back on it, she wasn't seeing me. I think she could have just plugged me in for any image right there—everyone had a story they were trying to live out—like they were in the middle of redefining themselves from who they really were. She started rolling a joint, but asked the driver first if it was okay. Can't remember what his face looked like, but I remember his apathetic responses.

The radio had one of the tracks from *Jazzmatazz* playing. "Loungin'," I think. We drove down Market Street smoking and listening to era-defining music while the world around us existed but mattered not. Market ran like a hammer down the center of the city, while the cab moved in and out from all of the trains and buses that tried to stay in the stream of concrete. Funny how different it was inside of a car.

She knew the one street to turn left on that would lead us to the spot in Chinatown she wanted to go. Zoomed past the daytime buildings that held workers who visited my new roommates' sex dungeon—they were, at that time, now home with their wives and children, away from their jobs and second lives of getting beat down.

The cab let us out in front of a spot in Chinatown. She tipped the guy well and gave him the rest of the joint, which he put out in his ashtray and saved for later.

Back into the night for him to finish work.

Into the spot for us, which was filled with locals. Her body was outlined so perfectly now. Remember thinking how cool she was and how amazing I felt to be the one she was with.

She talked to the waiter in Chinese and was ordering for us before we even got to the table. Seemed a little rude to me, but who was I to say what was proper and what was not. This beautiful woman is sitting across from me acting like she owns the place—telling the waiters to do this and that. Dishes slapping down on the tables are rattling like the train that used to come through Kansas City before moving across the rest of the country. Remembered my pops then and the stories he would tell me about what his father told him about the railroads. I'm pretty sure that the people working in this restaurant had grandfathers who would have told you much different stories about the railroads.

The wall behind her was made of mirror, and I caught a glimpse of myself, though I wish I hadn't. My mouth was wide open with a clown smile painted on without the paint.

Looked at Jenny and saw her chewing on a piece of gum like a cow chomps away at a piece of cud. An old couple next to us—who must have been married for at least thirty years, because they didn't talk but reacted perfectly to each other's movements—looked at us, then at each other, then back to their plates that had exactly the same amount of food on them.

Shouldn't have checked out my reflection.

The waiter brought the food that she had ordered—two bowls of this steaming soup, two small bowls of rice, and a plate stacked with some meat I couldn't identify. She took the gum from her rotating jaw that now seemed to grow in length and stuck it under the table—which the waiter saw. Without waiting for me, she started inhaling soup like her lip was a straw and making sucking sounds so disturbing that any remaining pleasant high I might have been feeling vanished. She then grabbed the little bowl of rice and brought it up just below her lips and started shoveling in the what-kind-of-meat-is-that? meat into her face, talking all the while:

"This is the best way to eat. Just live it up and don't wait. You have to indulge and just take in everything. I'm not waiting for manners or what people tell me to do, right? I'm just going to take it all in whenever I can. This is the life I've chosen, I don't know about you."

Still hadn't taken a bite. Her rate of consumption was astounding.

"I feel that way about men, too. You know, I've been fucking this guy Colby for a few weeks now and he won't even call me to see if he can come over—he just knocks on the door and thinks

I'm going to lay down for him. Right now, right now—hold on—"
She was trying to talk, but the air she needed for any sound to
come out was blocked by mounds of rice, meat, and soup. "So
right now, like I said, I'm just taking it all in. That's what I'm
about."

Realized then that everybody around us could hear what she
was saying because she was shouting over herself to be heard.
Felt small like a cartoon on the other end of a long dining table.
Looked at her in the mirror, thinking I would see the same pretty
girl that I had seen back at Handle's house, but that image had
fallen away. Was I even there in her mind or just something
else she was considering inhaling at some point in the evening?
Everyone was inhaling right then—taking in as much as they
possibly could. The slurping was too much.

Excused myself to go to the bathroom, but headed straight
out the door and onto the late-night Chinatown streets with an
empty stomach but not an ounce of appetite.

Now Chinatown in San Francisco is right next to North
Beach, the Italian section of the city. Crossed over the imaginary border and started walking up the slightly inclined street of
Columbus, not looking for anything but distance from what just
was. Walked until I got to City Lights Bookstore, the place where
everything started in the world that I was trying to get into but
could never. Stood in the alley that they renamed Jack Kerouac
Alley, and felt peace under the lamppost. Everything I enjoyed
took place fifty years ago and could only be looked back on and
never experienced.

Walked into City Lights. They hadn't built the poetry room
upstairs, so if you wanted to hear the creak of old wood, you'd
have to go downstairs where all of the history and politics
existed. Now, there are ghosts everywhere in San Francisco, I
guess because when they die they'd rather stick around than go

up to heaven. It's a great place to die, and here I was trying to save my father's life.

Sat wherever I could and either read or just watched everyone else look around. There were always cute girls with interesting bags looking for some words of wisdom to guide them through these times where they understood their bodies but they had to deal with boys who just didn't.

Are we ever the same age as each other?

After an hour or so, I walked out into the street with the faint sounds of John Coltrane following me, but those quickly faded away with each step.

Walking up Columbus, I found myself in front of Steps of Rome, a café spot run by Italians who just kept bringing their relatives over to work behind the counter. Found Colin sitting in front talking to the new waitress. We usually ran into each other around here. We could only afford the coffee, but the view was amazing. Just sitting on the sidewalk on a San Francisco evening, we were all out of place to be sure, but it didn't matter.

"Where'd you roll out to?" Colin asked. "Handle gets a little paranoid when people just vanish on him."

"I tried to get with that girl," I told him. "But she turned into a beast on me, so now I'm here with you fools again."

Colin smiled a little and kicked out a chair for me to sit in while he mixed the tip of his smoke with some herb.

We sat and talked loud for hours, then got edgy, so we made our way down the block, turned two dollars each into quarters, and headed towards the Lusty Lady, where Nick was standing outside trying to get some of the girls to go home with him.

It's funny that the underbelly of North Beach is not all that dirty when you look at it from the outside. The Lusty Lady was a strange spot to go to, now that I think about it, and we went often. It was a strip club, but not like the kind you see in the movies—though I'm not sure what kind of movies you watch. There were individual booths that you walked into, closed the door, and dropped quarters in—which triggered a window to open that revealed a room full of naked girls dancing around. Only one of the rooms had a one-way window. The rest were just glass, so when yours opened, one of the girls would come over and start dancing in front of your window. The key would be to stack the quarters on the ledge of the window without actually touching anything.

The room they danced in was meant to be like an ancient harem, with pillows and lace all around. The back wall was all mirror, which was supposed to make the room look bigger, but if you looked at it, you could see all of the little faces of the men watching the women dance.

The girl dancing in front of me looked familiar—but underneath her brunette wig, I couldn't place her, until she tripped over one of the pillows and I saw the tattoo on top of her bald head and I recognized her from my roommate's show. Saw the history of her and what she must have gone through to end up here. There were levels of strippers in the city—the sex industry was like any other, you see. High-class whores, sex dungeon folks like those I lived with, and the working class, who made decent cash but not enough to get out, and certainly not enough to support the drug habits they needed to keep their maximum earning potential going.

Back out to the streets, Nick was just waking up and talking about meeting the sun. Let them convince me that I would be missing something if I just went home and crashed. You need to be careful of people who tell you that adventure exists at the next turn—because it turns out that they are not really walking into a story, but running away from a history that chases them throughout time.

2.

Was standing in the middle of people at some club having fun and throwing themselves about without a care. Should have stayed out under that lamppost in the alley of City Lights, figuring out how I was going to get paid.

Had been leaving people and places all night long, so I toughed it out, thinking that Nick was edgy like me and would want to jump, but I was wrong because he hooked up with a girl, so I just sat on the couch and watched as people groped each other.

Again, those guys with the black polo shirts were walking around, this time shadowing girls and skinny boys who were handing out energy drinks for them. Each person who took a bottle got their picture taken by one of the men in black polo shirts while holding the gender of their preference and a free drink.

Walked over to the window and looked out over the city. There was weight to it. Made my way down the stairs and back into the streets, opening the door and getting a piece of the silence of the city. Alone again and comfortable without the knowledge of anything else going on around me.

Insulated.

City was full of homeless and kids running around tagging up whatever they could.

Walked those streets because it was my joy back then.

Had no idea what time it was when I got to the steps and stood under the clamshell. On the stoop, one of the kids who lived in the apartment on the first floor was listening to music that wasn't playing anywhere. He was tweaked out of his mind and praying that the sun wouldn't come up too soon. Maybe he wasn't thinking that at all, though—he might not have been thinking anything. He might have just been sitting there doing what he wanted. Lucky.

Tired for the first time all evening.

Victor was a DJ or something at some club, or was at least trying to be. He kept asking me to do a zine on him.

Up the stairs and into the living room with the open doors that led into the kitchen. The goat-faced boy Kurt was sitting at the table eating a bowl of cereal and I decided to join him, but found that wasn't possible because it was the end of both my milk and cereal on the table in front of him.

"Sorry," he said with my Golden Grahams falling out of his mouth. "I figured you'd be out all night and I'd just pick you up some in the morning before you got back."

Sat across the table from him and watched him eat the last of my cereal. He was whispering when he talked to me and grunted in between scoops.

"Marcy's asleep, so I want to keep it like that," he said. "She wore me out today. Plus I had some work, so it was a double day. No time to go out and do anything I need to do. Tell me about your night?"

"Bad date. Then to a club with some friends but had to get out of there. Things just weren't feeling right. Been leaving places all night, actually."

"We're always leaving somewhere, Sarah, except when we die. The trick is to learn to enjoy where you're at and make the most of that—then you can always get comfortable when the situation becomes tense. You'll rarely see me freak out."

With that, he put the spoon on the table, drank the last drop of the milk with the sugary bottom, and lit up a menthol. He looked comfortable all right, and smiled because he enjoyed what he just told me. After putting his feet up on the table, I noticed that his socks were like new.

Saw me looking at the socks and offered me one of his smokes. "Hope you don't mind, I just didn't have a chance to do any laundry today. You're like me, though—clean socks make the night."

The steps sounded with boots.

Could hear Valerie stomp heavy up the stairs. She looked around quickly and noticed us at the table, came in and smiled, never taking her bag off her shoulder or putting down the plastic bag of groceries that she was carrying.

"How was work?" I asked.

She smiled at the normalcy of the question.

"Pretty good today actually, though I had to take this guy into the back room for like an hour. He was a mess, just talking about his job and what he should or shouldn't have done throughout the day. I thought about what I was going to make for dinner while I was on top of him, though, and came up with something good."

She held up her bag of groceries just as Darren D. came racing down the stairs that led into the living room, looking like a dog that had been waiting all day for his owner to come and take him out. He half smiled, grabbed her purse, and went slowly upstairs before stopping halfway.

"I'll get it all ready, okay?" he said.

"Sure, that's what I was thinking," Valerie replied after exhaling. "I'm coming." She dropped the bag of groceries on the table and followed him upstairs.

Before she reached the top of the stairs, she stopped and turned to me.

"I almost forgot—this guy kept talking about that he needed smart young kids—clean kids, though—to line up and work.

Said the money was going to be great. Starting up company. Something with computers. You interested?"

"What do I know about computers?"

"You do your zine, right? They need someone who knows computers. The old folks out there have no idea. You know computers? I told him you did."

"Not really," I said. "I don't even use the ones at Kinko's. Enjoy the direction connection between my hands and what I make."

"It's never what you know, it's how you present yourself to someone you need money from."

She handed me the card, and my heart moved a bit because I saw in her eyes that this exchange—that this piece of doing something—mattered to her. Perhaps she spent so much time exchanging services for money, it was a treat to be able to act on her own will. Before the moment could extend, she bounced up the stairs.

"He didn't even say hello to her," I said. "What a dick."

"She'll return the favor, don't worry about that," the goat-faced boy said. "Everything changes pretty quick."

His smirk faded away when Marcy came out of their room, wiping her eyes and clapping her tongue to the roof of her mouth.

"Where'd you go? I got scared."

The little girl voice that she used did not go with her large frame and faded green Manic Panic hair dye. Kurt got up and disappeared when he tried to put his arms around her. She moved his hand into hers and led him and my socks into their bedroom.

Walked upstairs, sat in the middle of the ballroom, and just looked out over the city that had been holding me all night. Played a Dexter Gordon album and did nothing but get up and turn the record over when it was time.

Paws scraped the floor to announce the coming of Valerie and Darren D.'s wolf dog, followed by his owners. Both of them were calm and friendly when they approached softly.

"It's the best time right now," Valerie said. "After work, with hours to go before the next shift and the useless part of the city asleep. It's like everything is for us."

She had showered and was now in sweats with a towel over her head. Unless she smiled, you couldn't tell she was a vampire. Darren D., lost in a thought, positioned himself in front of the window so that it provided a reflection for him to see his fangs.

"I wish there really wasn't a reflection," he said, squinting his eyes in an attempt to make it real.

Both of them were nodding their heads to the music and admiring the same scene. The wolf dog sat in front and completed the picture.

Here, with the vampires and the wolf, was the moment I had been looking for all evening.

CHAPTER 4

i.

The young couple who had just moved in reminded me of the people back home I had never gotten along with but tried so hard to understand. They were just married—either that or they just were on their way.

Moved in with their boxes and neat little plastic containers thinking that this was the start of their San Francisco life together. He was a teacher down in Hunter's Point—one of those brave souls who really believed he could make a difference in the world. They'd both finished their master's degrees and were about to start receiving steady paychecks.

The borrowing that took place over food and clothes turned out to get to them more than it got to me. Remember when they had a locksmith come over and put a deadbolt on their door and thinking how silly it was, because if you didn't like what was going on in the house, you should just leave.

Crazy was the norm, and if you weren't, people looked at you as if you were the freak.

Everyone was pretty close in the house at this time. Was no longer the newbie there, and felt comfortable with the vampires, the goat-faced boy, and even the goat-faced boy's fag hag, who still got her rocks off because she had money coming in from her mom and dad, though that was being stretched too far.

At work, the café was losing so much business. The owners were taking way too much money out of the register, and that, coupled with the free food that we were taking plus what I was giving to my friends and trading for mix tapes, was putting us in debt beyond belief. On one Sunday, with the sky turning dark blue, the two brothers came in while their dates for the night sat in the back seat of the old Caddie parked in front. My pops would have known the year of that car. From what I could see, they were two cute Rockabilly girls waiting to be taken out on a nice night after a bunch of so-so nights with guys their own age who could only afford food that you eat with your hands.

"We're going to have to shut it down," the older one said—the one who was better looking than the other. "We've been losing too much. It was a fun ride, and I'm glad we tried. Thanks for sticking it out."

"How long until we close?" I asked, adding up the money I had in my bank account.

"Today is the last day," the uglier of the two brothers said. "But we're not closing. We actually got a cool offer and are getting bought out. All the smaller shops around here are getting offers, too. This is actually one of the few they're going to keep functioning as a café. The rest they're just tearing down to eliminate the competition. Sucks, huh?"

I looked over to the better looking one—the one who used to be punk rock and rebel against "the system," but had let his brother fill his nose with coke and sit him in the back of a sweet ride with hot girls. His eyes looked inward and fell.

The car horn honked, and the two looked back like their necks had been lassoed by a rodeo clown.

"You can close down early if you like," the ugly one said as he opened the register and took out the big bills. "We'll take care of cleaning up later. There's people coming in. Also, if a man named Freddy comes by, give him the spare set of keys. He's going to be taking over the rent come Monday."

He stuffed the wad of cash from the register into his pocket, turned up his collar, and walked with his brother toward their dates and classic moments about to be. Don't remember if I locked up or just walked right out the door into the soon-to-be night. The Mission District changed during that time—the transition. Always walking through transitions but never ending up in movements.

2.

My friend Lina, who worked at the café when I first started but left because she fell for the charm of one of the brothers, lived close to there—Twenty-fourth and Capp Street—so I headed over to have something to drink and try not to think about how I was going to find more work. People were struggling to find jobs. Remembered how many people had come into the café looking for work—now they had a head start on me because they had already been to the places I was going to go to. Had that business card that Valerie had handed me, but what the hell did I know about computers or working in offices?

Had to land a gig before calling my pops again. Kept hearing my mother's voice, holding back crying. That's tough, you know—when they put it on you to bring in the cash and you haven't yet figured out how to do that, exactly.

Lina was there, but so was the new boy she was dating. He had set himself up pretty good—already had his Super Nintendo plugged into her TV and was running through a season of Madden.

Used their phone to call back to the house to let everyone know that I wouldn't be bringing any leftovers home and that they'd have to fend for themselves, but the guy from the new couple answered the phone, and he didn't sound happy.

"They sold my TV," he said, nearly in tears. "I'm going to burn this place down! This is hell, and I'm leaving you ALL here to rot. Enjoy."

Teachers are kind of high-strung, but I don't blame them. Couldn't imagine trying to do the impossible all day long with a class of forty kids all working against you, only to come home to find male hookers noshing on your Hostess cupcakes.

Hearing someone having a worse day than me lightened my mood.

Lina cheered as her boyfriend scored a game-winning touchdown by using the Houston Oilers' vicious passing attack, sending his buddy pacing around the room. When he turned around, I noticed him right away—the boy with the flyer at Kinko's.

His anger over losing the football game faded when he looked at me. It was nice to be the object of someone else's pleasure.

"How goes the revolution?" I asked. "This must be a tune-up for when you all take the streets."

"Strategy," he laughed. "All strategy."

"You two totally know each other, right?" Lina beamed. "That's just so perfect. Alberto's always got something heavy to say, and I could use something to lighten him up. Sarah, you're just the cure for that."

"You got any new mags?" I asked her, not wanting to deal with how hard Alberto was trying not to blush. I was into boys, but not *blushing* into them.

Lina and I went into her room, and I lay on her bed, shuffling through all of her mags. She had lifetime subscriptions to about fifteen magazines because she won some high-level spelling bee in Sacramento when she was thirteen sponsored by Condé Nast or someplace like that.

"So don't play like you don't want to know all about Alberto," she said, pushing me over to a half roll. "Alberto Orca!"

"What's to know? I saw him printing out some flyers, trying to start up a protest or something like that. Mind if I take some of these pages? Could use some pictures."

We both smiled, and she held out a bit before giving in.

"He's a bike messenger with Allen—well, until Allen finishes law school. He graduates this year. I think he's going to ask me to marry him! Anyhow, Alberto is kind of a legend in his own way. Been a messenger for ten years and knows all the routes of the city. He tried to unionize them, actually, but they busted it when he got too close. You can take whatever you like if you come with us today. Fun is a part of life too, right?"

"Right now, I'm interested in making some money, that's all," I said, looking at a pair of Chucks on a model who shouldn't have been wearing them. "Can I use your phone?"

"Sure," she said, jumping off the bed. "You can have all the mags, too. Just come with us down to Pescadero. We got some shrooms. Crazy Leon is coming over now and we're going to hit the beach. There's enough for you if you want to join."

"I've never done those before," I told her. "That might be a little hardcore for me. See enough in reality as it is."

"Nah, it's not acid," she pleaded. "Besides, you made Alberto soften a little bit, and the last thing I want to hear about when I'm trippin' on the beach with my baby is how the drug companies are about to take control of the world."

"Are they?" I asked.

"Who cares!" She smiled—not wide, but warm.

"Sarah, you're rolling with us," Lina's boyfriend yelled. "My boy Alberto needs not to feel like a third wheel."

A car honked downstairs.

"Crazy Leon has arrived," Allen said, putting on his jacket and beanie. "You better bundle up yourself, cutie, it's going to a cold night out there on the sandy dunes!"

Lina loaned me a jacket that was too big, and we left down to the awaiting ride—Lina on Allen's lap in shotgun, Crazy Leon at the wheel, and me and Alberto in the back seat with a shockingly clear look at Mr. Crazy Leon's eyes in the rearview mirror.

"I've been thinking about this all day," Crazy Leon stated. "I'm really out to lose all sense of pride today. All of you should know that before we take off."

Alberto leaned forward and tossed in his Del *I Wish My Brother George Was Here* tape. The car started up, and we were headed away from the city and out towards the beaches that stretched below the 101 as it headed south.

The music was righteous. Liked Alberto right away and was attracted enough to him, but it wasn't burning inside of me.

3.

It felt comfortable when the night took over. Not so much the night, but the period of dusk. All of the thoughts that haunt you and drive you into constant questioning just faded away as the winding roads of the coast gripped Crazy Leon and his beat-up old Honda. We had eaten all of the caps a few minutes back, thinking that our destination was almost ready for us.

Kept looking at the tape deck in front while Alberto leaned forward at the end of each song and switched from the first Cyprus Hill album, to Bran Nubian, to the Pharcyde, until he finally settled on Primus's *Frizzle Fry*. I guess it was the right choice—as soon as the bass kicked in, the tape deck that I was concentrating on started smiling. Rain that I hadn't noticed before drummed the roof. Lines in my hands started to deepen. It was a little too much for me, but everyone else seemed to be okay with it, so I just bent down a little in the back seat and turned up towards Alberto.

"Shhhh," I said. "Don't let anyone know what's going on. It might affect how Leon's driving."

"I won't tell anyone." Alberto smiled. "I think everyone knows anyhow, though. We're good."

The car swerved a bit, but the music stayed on point.

"What! What do we know?" screamed Leon, looking back at us in the rearview mirror, then twisting and turning it so he could see us. "If you know something you better tell me, because I'm in control of this thing here and we need to get to our beach in the right way. Everything is fine. You can tell me that."

"We're all fine," Alberto said, popping out the Primus and tossing in some Charlie Parker to calm down the mood. Amazing that so much time had passed in the world of American music that Charlie Parker would now be considered mellow. The saxophone guided us, along with Crazy Leon, to our spot at Pescadero Beach, and a release from the car. Moms had all those old records, but could only listen to them once Dad fixed the player.

Leon got out and took a huge breath of the ocean air. Alberto kept on changing the tapes in the car even though no more music was coming out.

"Come on," I said. "Check out those birds against the black mosaic. I know—I know it's hard to let go of all the bullshit you feel responsible for, but I hereby relieve you from all of this, for this night at least. After all, I need somebody to escort me."

Don't know what my body was doing, but my mind was looking at the sky and marveling at how many different forms of night it was starting to become. How white the birds were. Might have been stars. Everything was moving.

The beaches of Northern California are rocky and rough. We walked out to the tip and looked out over the ocean. Guess there was a twenty-five-foot drop that led down to the beach, which we managed to get down without any worries of time or technique. Allen wasn't talking at all.

Finally on the beach, the five of us looked out to the ocean, standing not too far behind a group of rocks that took the brunt of the waves. There were red lights reflecting off of them—which I thought nothing of, seeing as how the rest of the world around me made little sense compared to how I usually saw it.

Lina jumped up on the rock and threw her arms into the sky.

"Come on, I challenge you to be greater than I am! Can you beat the humans?"

While she yelled at the ocean, Crazy Leon bent over and slapped his knees with a loud laugh and monstrous roar of enjoyment. He looked like a toy whose spring would never stop. Alberto put his hand on Allen's shoulder and said something to the effect of, "These are the moments we'll remember," but Allen brushed it away, not wanting anything to come inside of his protective bubble. He pointed at his headphones and nodded slowly.

A wave came crashing up against the rock and nearly pulled Lina into the ocean on its retreat. She screamed and Leon echoed it. Allen was silent.

"Did you see it?" Lina said, pulling herself up from the wet sand. "They tried to take me back with them, but I wasn't having it. I wanted to stay with you all. We're family. I'm not leaving that for an ocean adventure!"

The red lights became heavier and heavier. Could hear sounds telling me we weren't supposed to be there. Those voices started getting louder and were out of place in the moment.

Alberto walked in front of me and nodded up towards the cliff we'd just walked down from. Could barely make out the car—then could see the black-and-white, and then the policeman standing in front of it.

"You can't be down there," the voice boomed again, this time clear. "The beach closed five minutes ago. Time to leave."

Lina dusted herself off but couldn't get clean enough. Alberto nodded at Crazy Leon, telling him with his eyes to act cool around the cop once we got to the car. The rocks on the bottom of the beach started turning to skulls, but I had no time to pay attention to that and made a note to myself to talk with Alberto about it later.

Back on the road was the place we had to go but least wanted to be.

Got to the top and saw that the cop was more of a ranger than a cop, but the image of who he seemed to be was more imposing than who he actually was.

"Time to go, folks, it's not safe down there after dark. Looks like I rescued your friend there just in time," he said, pointing at Lina and her drenched body.

Crazy Leon looked normal while opening the door and starting up the ride. We all slunk in and said nothing. Alberto put in something, though I can't recall what it was. All I heard was the engine turn on—and with that, leaving the ranger waving at us in the background, we were kicking into full bloom with our trip and driving down a twisting highway with rain falling all around us, looking for a port that had yet to be discovered.

So much for plans.

We were in it now. Drove slow on the highway, in the rain, through the night, looking for a place to pull over.

Crazy Leon turned around and didn't look all that crazy right then. He was calm and ready to deliver his cargo to a safe place. He didn't want to waste his trip looking for a parking space, but he realized that the responsibility thrust upon him would answer those in his past who might have questioned his dedication to discipline.

Indeed.

"What we need to do is stay calm," he said, even-toned. "So keep it low and we'll be good. Any noise is going to distract the course. Are well all aboard with our captain? Nod if you understand."

We all nodded, said nothing, and put our trust in the man behind the wheel. The skulls I saw in the sand of the beach duplicated themselves in the cliffs next to us as we drove, which was a little disheartening because the cliffs weren't fully exposed, so every once in a while an oncoming headlight would illuminate something terrible next to us. It was better to just stay in the dark and listen to our good captain.

Leon saw an opening on the side of the road, did a slightly risky U-turn, and pulled off. There were no signs on that little space of land that looked over the unmarked beach, but there were other cars there as well, so the reasoning was that it would be safe. The engine stopped, and we got out onto the sand.

Rain was coming down at such an alarming rate we all must have been soaked, but nobody was paying attention to what was wrong with the situation—only that we had survived and were now safe. A flock of birds in front of us moved like a painting that kept splitting apart and then coming back together. Allen balled up in his puffy coat and looked extremely comfortable, while Lina was, I think, having another go with the ocean, but this time in a more conversational mode.

Crazy Leon was basking in the glow of getting his crew to safety, and he flicked his long hair every which way so that he looked like a freaked-out version of one of those shampoo commercials. He drew a line in front of himself in the sand and looked back with a giant grin. He kept faking jumping over it. Stood up and walked right over that line and he just lost it—cheering like he had just watched his boyhood baseball team hit the game winner in the World Series.

Thought of my dad watching the Cardinals win the World Series in '83—he grabbed me so tight and spun me around when Lonnie Smith came sliding in headfirst on the steal of home.

Crazy Leon snapped his fingers like he remembered something and pulled a tennis ball from inside his pocket.

"Grab a bat," he said through his laugh. "You crossed the line, which means you're up. You two, get out there and play the field. We've got a game."

Alberto trotted to where centerfield would have been, and Lina went over to third base—Allen behind the plate to be the umpire.

The moon outside looked like the last stadium light still on, but it was more than enough for us. Stars (or birds) were flashbulbs from the photographers.

Leon was very careful not to step across the line he was using as a pitcher's mound. Saw a piece of wood that seemed to have a Sarah Striker signature calling out to me and started taking warm-up swings while they tossed the ball around. He looked in to his catcher, shook off a couple of signs, and tossed a wicked curve. Swung and missed badly and the ball rolled past the imaginary catcher. He started screaming at me to run—that this was my chance. A crowd grew from the rocks and sand, echoing the crashing waves with thunderous chants and claps, so I took off around the bases. The crowd transformed. Skulls again. Alberto was laughing silently, holding in the noise but letting his chest puff out and in. They were all waving me home, and soon they too rounded the bases with me. We were at the peak of enjoyment, there, in the rain, with nothing but ourselves to provide life. It was amazing. We all crossed home together and celebrated the victory.

The flock of birds moved again, their flapping wings echoing cheers from the ocean. All fell silent except the sounds of rain against our coats.

Allen, who had yet to say a word, was pointing at something in the background, back towards where we had left the car. It was a giant yellow sign—something familiar.

"What? What is it?" Crazy Leon yelled. "What are you pointing at?!"

"Denny's!" Alberto said. "It's a Denny's."

Crazy Leon busted out laughing, his eyes bigger than the moon that was doing its best to peek though the cloud bed over the ocean. "You're crazy. You want to go *in* there? You want to go in there. YOU WANT TO GO IN THERE!"

We all walked through the heavy sand and up to the parking lot. Crazy Leon held the door open for us as we all walked through. The warmth we felt reminded us how cold and wet we were.

"Five, please," Alberto said in his best sane voice. "We'll need a table that fits five."

The hostess, a young local girl who no doubt had had her own adventures on the beach, showed us kindness and a table in a section that had been closed. "I think it might be best if you sat here," she said. "I'll take care of you."

Leon lost it and starting laughing like a hyena. What could we do? The man had held it together for us throughout the hard times of the night, and here, among people having their evening meals, it was his time to let it go. We all shuffled into our private section and sloshed down into the booth, opened up the menus, and started in with the task of ordering something to eat.

Everyone else struggled to speak their orders and did their best to point to a picture on the menu. As soon as I saw the grilled cheese sandwich, I was good.

Alberto was having a little trouble choosing.

"I'll split mine with him," I told the waitress, handing her both of our menus.

"You two are kind of cute together," she said.

All of a sudden, from complete silence, Allen started freestyling right there.

The faces of the parents seated around us turned sour, but none of us wanted to stop Allen, as these were his first words in hours. The rest of the waitresses around us were seeing their evening tips flying away, while the one who had taken care of us was now whispering something to the line cook—a giant man whose body looked like it was in constant competition with his T-shirt.

The cook came out from behind the counter and walked up to us holding his spatula. Allen would not let his flow be interrupted, but he gave way when the metal hit the table and the chef's eyes looked bold at us. Anything could have happened at that moment, which was exciting in its own right. Remember thinking that this evening was turning into something epic.

The cook stood up, his muscles now turning to a comic book level of big, and started rapping. I don't remember exactly what he said—nobody was paying attention to the words at the start, only the actions, but we soon realized it was all about being in prison and what he went through.

> *Warden lines you up with the injection*
> *That's how it's handled*
> *Departmental Corrections*
> *Sold like slaves down rivers of pills*
> *Cost some their lives to get you that refill.*

He twirled his spatula and walked back to the kitchen. We were silent again—not sure anything else was said for the remainder of the meal. We all aged a bit there.

We eventually paid, cleaned ourselves off, and headed back to the car to drive into the city and get some rest. Crazy Leon didn't even attempt to drive, just put the keys on top of the car and headed to the back seat. There was a huge smile on his face— such a look of satisfaction. Alberto shook his head no and went into the back seat with him.

Lina looked at me.

"I'm not really the best candidate for this one," I said. "I'm not seeing right."

"I've got no license," she said. "So, considering the state everyone is in, while you may not be in the best shape when talking about the rest of the world, for this moment, you're the one."

She tossed me the keys and got into the passenger's seat.

Getting in and turning on the ignition was a task in itself. Once I got the car started and took a few breaths, the silence of the outside coupled with the noise from the engine did nothing but heighten my nerves. The tape player had been overworked and had our Leaders of the New School stuck inside. Had to have something playing in the background.

Allen finally reacted.

"Well, welcome back, friends," he started in. "What a game we have underway. It's the bottom of the fifth and the action has been nonstop. Sarah Striker has been pitching an amazing game so far despite a rocky start. She's hung in there and limited the damage, but now is facing the heart of their lineup and they've already seen her twice."

Lina's smile let me know why she was so into this guy.

"The bullpen has been heavily worked, so it's up to her Let's see how she works it. Goodman's first up, and he's hungry for a hit. Been struggling all year, so facing the curves and sliders of this young pitcher is going to be tough."

The car pulled away and damn if Allen didn't keep going all the way back to the city. He announced the entire game as the colors of the coast showed themselves. The rain ended and the sun came up while we listened to the greatest ball game of all time being announced right next to me—a memory that will never leave my soul.

I reached back across the country and felt Pops sitting at the kitchen table watching a replay of the game. Then, I understood that family exists inside of you regardless of your location on the planet. Tried to get deeper on that, but there was still a game to finish. Pops would have enjoyed watching—so I lent him my eyes to do so.

We dipped into the city as it was coming alive, but the game was ending for us. Getting over a bases-loaded jam in the bottom of the ninth, Alberto rushed the mound and the crowd went wild as we pulled up in front of the Capp Street house, leaving Leon in the car to sleep it all off.

CHAPTER 5

i.

Everyone was sitting in a circle for our house meeting. Well, not everyone. The young couple who had moved in not too long ago were going as fast as they could up and down the stairs, not really taking too much care if their belongings got damaged. Don't think their stay in San Francisco was a good one.

We needed someone to move in fast. Saturdays we were usually all together. Kurt looked a little worn out from whatever he'd gotten into the night before; guess that client's demands were a little more intense than just watching bees and collecting herb. Marcy was twitching and nervous, rubbing Kurt's leg where he didn't want it rubbed. The two vamps were mellow and in sweatpants and biker shorts, though I wish that Darren D. would have worn the sweats. Valerie looked amazing without any makeup on.

"We need to pull in some money," Marcy said. "Especially with those two leaving now. Maybe we could throw a party."

Valerie looked at me and smiled with her fangs nicely brushed. "Come on, let's ask her," she said, scooting over to me like a high school girl about to share her lunch. "We want to set up a dungeon here," she said to me. "It would bring in some serious cash and save us the rent we're spending on other places and time. Time is most important."

"Dungeon?" I asked, taking a bite of my Pop-Tart. "How's that?"

"Well, the house is totally fit for it. I have my own clients—all of us in some way have our own clients, right?"

They all nodded. Remember looking around at them and realizing that we were in a house meeting talking about whether or not to start up a sex dungeon in the place where we lived. This was not talk about who should buy toilet paper or working out a schedule for washing dishes.

"We think it would be great," Darren D. added in. "We've been talking. You know, I have a few guys who I could bring in—and Val, well, she has people and connections at the O'Farrell—right?" (Valerie nodded, proud.)

"People are always asking me if I have anyplace special," the goat-faced boy added. "We could totally get our house cleaned for free! See, I have this one guy who will come in twice a week and be our maid. He likes to clean in his leather suit and really sweat. You can yell at him and beat him if you like, but don't hit him too hard. If you do, he'll just keep breaking dishes and we won't have anything left."

"We thought you'd be the whip girl," Valerie finally blurted out like it was the payoff, something I'd been waiting to hear. "You won't have to do anything sexual at all. But, you know, we think you're kind of good-looking—a little clean-cut in that tomboy-with-the-sexy-Louise-Brooks-hair kind of way—so that could put a nice spin on things. We'd give you a full share. You'd just have to get people ready by giving them a few lashes. What do you think?"

What did I think?

"What if my friends came over and saw me as a whip girl?" I said. "It might give them the wrong idea. Sorry. Don't be mad."

They weren't mad—but they'd just heard money being drained from their plans.

"You sure?" Valerie asked. "This could really help the house out. We know what we're doing. I know you're short on cash—this is the alternative to going into an office and working. Believe me, this is a better gig. Did you call that guy about the job yet? I'm sure you didn't because I know you. You're more like me than you want to believe. You're not cut out for that life—nobody really is, they just convince themselves they are or that they need to be. You have a choice."

Can't say that I didn't think about that, and think hard on it. Would have been good to take the easy money and go down the road of being the whip girl in the sex dungeon house. Could have done a whole book on that, had I lived through it.

Tell you the truth, it wasn't really the physical part of it all that made me turn it down. It was purely financial.

There might have been some artistic merit to it and I would have learned a few things, but most of those things I'd learned anyway just by being around the people I was living with—not sure I wanted any more of that.

Looked at all of them and saw that they had accumulated nothing—that's not what I was about. I had to stack cash for my pops and make enough for me to live and not get lost in the world doing it. Not a chance.

Long money is always the best bet. Short cash leaves you short-changed, broke, and looking for people to whip.

Right then, something inside of me went off. Started thinking about how to get out of there. Planning my escape.

> *Thinkin' of a master plan*
> *Cuz ain't nuthin' but sweat inside my hand*
> *So I dig into my pocket, all my money is spent*
> *So I dig deeper but still comin' up with lint*
>
> *—Rakim*

Only thing was, I had no job and was broke myself, but there was no way I was going to be anyone's whip girl—I don't care what kind of story it made. Was sure that my pops at that kitchen table back home would be shaking his head no on that one, and since he didn't do that often, I'd have to listen.

Now, though, I had to toughen up and not show my thoughts. When you're weak, show 'em you're strong.

"We'll figure something out," I said. "We need to get someone else to move in here and take that room. Nobody can afford the extra rent."

The human tolerance for what becomes normal is astonishing.

2.

Looking for a job in San Francisco.

Knew that if I was going to move out of the house, I needed some cash for first and last somewhere else. Didn't want to play the card yet that Valerie had given me because, to this point, though I was short on cash, debt had yet to creep up. Always more time to move without that around your neck.

In the early mornings, I'd sit somewhere and read a paper and look through the want ads for work—circling jobs that sounded like they would pay me. The physical act of sitting there with a newspaper made me feel engaged.

Chose jobs that had a telephone number to call because I couldn't afford a fax. In those days, you still had to call people and either set up an interview or mail them your résumé. Everything was a physical experience—something you could touch and feel and be a part of. You were creating extensions of yourself all over the place.

Circled an ad that read: "Wanted: telephone salespeople. Cash paid. Work 6-10, make 10 dollars an hour plus commission. Classic work and an honest day's pay."

It was there and perfect. Called the man on the other end of the line, made an appointment for around five o'clock, and that was that. He told me that if everything went well, I'd be working that very evening. Felt good. Money coming would allow for an escape from that house. Then I could bounce and get something better.

Started strolling up and down the back hills of the city. Fell in love with various people who were working on the other side of windows. Thought about visiting Alberto on the messenger wall, but boys get the wrong impression if you just drop in on them. Didn't need anyone falling in love with me.

There was no urge to go down to the Lusty Lady in the middle of the day—it wasn't the same.

Walked up a side hill and saw a man standing on a box tossing up the bird to the camera of a woman who was busy snapping photos of him. The woman saw me notice her and smiled a little. She mouthed something to me I couldn't understand. Tried it again. Still nothing.

"She's trying to tell you 'It's him!', okay?" the man said, then turned to the photographer. "Now, my lady, why don't we go finish off a bottle and do the rest of this in my apartment?" He popped his tongue in his cheek and jumped around on top of the milk crate he was posing on.

Then I saw. Somehow I don't know how I knew—I'm not sure even if I knew because I was looking more at the girl who was taking the pictures than at the old man she was taking pictures of. I knew it was him. Lawrence Ferlinghetti himself.

This man built the bookstore I haunted at every chance and created movements and published legends and was, in fact, himself a legend, though right then he was just another guy trying to get a girl to come back to his apartment.

Made me like him even more.

Lit up a smoke right there and thought of something to ask or say to him.

"You're trying to kill yourself," he said to me, getting down off the crate. "Pretty good way to go about it by putting that crap into your face."

Was shocked and felt like a stupid kid. That's how I quit cigarettes, if anyone really wants to know.

"I'm kind of a publisher as well, you know," I told him, perhaps expecting him to be thrilled or take me under his wing or something like that. "You have any advice for me?"

"Yeah—I do. Goes like this: Surround yourself with talented people who other people don't realize are so talented, and do whatever you can to get it out. Never believe what anyone tells you because those who have time to critique have little time to create."

He turned his attention back to the girl, who put her hand on his elbow more like he was her grandfather than a man she was thinking of. Wanted to ask him more or perhaps get to be his friend so that I would have some connection to him and the movement, but no words came out.

Continued through the city and had to kill about four hours of time before the interview. It's a small city if you have no direction to walk in.

3.

The interview was down in the Marina District, a place where thoughts of vampires and other such rock 'n' roll behavior just didn't exist. The Marina is where the normal people lived. Was happy to go down there and thought that by working around some sense of stability it might rub off on me. Money by association.

The office was on the second floor of a building that looked like the last dollhouse left on the shelf.

The man who interviewed me was tall, sported a heavy mustache and a regular haircut. He closed the door to the room in back of him, where people on the phones did their best to send looks at me through the closing door. There wasn't enough time to get a proper read on what they were trying to tell me. From what I could see inside, the place looked more like a living room than an office.

"So, you're probably wondering how a fellow like me becomes a chimney sweep," he said to me, smiling and looking at me, but a little more over my head than anywhere else. "Can you guess?"

"I really have no idea," I told him. "Not in the mood for games, only for a job."

"Well, this is me," he professed, handing me an eight-by-ten glossy photo. "You think you can sell this?"

The picture was him dressed up like a hobo carrying a broom and wearing a semi-ripped jacket and a faded top hat.

"I put on this outfit, drive out to people's houses, and clean out their chimneys. It's an old art—I'm pretty good at it. The folks, they all get a kick out of it—seeing me drive up and come out of the van in the outfit. The kids, they get a real hoot out of it.

"What I need are people to reach out to this list of people with chimneys in the area and ask if they are in need of my services. Pretty simple, actually. I give you five dollars an hour for sitting here making the call and twenty dollars for each appointment you book. No reason why you can't be making at least a hundred dollars a day here. Well, a night, actually."

Looked at him, then back at the picture, then at him again. Thought about the money and how that could really help in planning my escape from the vampires and prostitutes. All of that mixed up right then and my brain got convinced that this was a great way to make money. After all, how many people did this anymore? Yes, this would be my normal job: book appointments for a man to go clean people's chimneys. Wouldn't have to sell drugs anymore—could stay clean and have my days free for *Luddite*. Life was going to be fine.

Started that night. Looking back now, don't think I filled out any paperwork. The man promised me he'd pay me in cash. He did hand me a folder with some press clippings of himself and a few articles that had been written about him.

"I pay at the end of the month. Just an envelope of cash," he said. "If that works for you, then you should get on that phone and start working for me. The last three before you all got the same speech and took off. Scared about earning their own way. What about you?"

Got on the phone right away and started selling chimney sweeps.

First thing you need to know if you're going to sell chimney sweeps is about creosote. Creosote are flammable wood chips that build up in your chimney that can catch fire and burn your house down. Well, that's what he told me anyway, and that's the fear I sold. First time I learned how to sell fear, which would help me later. It was not that hard of a sell actually—if you had a fireplace, you were home and someone called telling you that if you didn't clean it out before the next time you snuggled up to your fire, the whole house could go up in flames, you'd at least listen.

Started out great—selling six appointments a night—which if you added it to my five bucks an hour would be getting me well over a hundred dollars in cash a day, five days a week. That's over two grand a month in cash, which at that time was still tons of money to live, eat, and move around. Be able to escape in a month. Until then, I'd lay as low as I could at the house, stay out until the late nights with my friends getting into madness around the city, document it in *Luddite*, and work for this man in the normal place in town selling chimney sweeps.

4.

Taking the 22 Fillmore bus—I can still remember hearing Too $hort being played from the back with kids wearing SF Giants ball caps with rhinestones laid over the logo. The cables attached to the back ran on electric wires that stretched through the city. When we stopped, there were no sounds of engines, only the people stirring about and the music going from those little boxes. There was no stereo sound, which is why I think that rap music from the Bay Area has that distinct tin.

Got home and saw the goat-faced boy in front of the building balancing his time between standing under the clamshell awning and stepping out into the sunshine to look up and down the block. He didn't notice me until I was next to him.

"Hey," he said, seeming to be spooked for a second before he started his looking again. "You going upstairs?"

"Sure," I told him. "You waiting for somebody?"

He didn't answer, but looked up to the window of our building and shook his head no at Marcy, who pointed at a man walking up the steep incline that I had just walked from. Kurt ran up to him with money clenched in his skinny hand, and I headed upstairs. Valerie was dressed for work and cooking something in the kitchen, but when I walked over to see a little closer, she was just moving an empty pan back and forth over the flame.

Reached in and turned it off.

"Thanks," she said. "Sometimes it's hard to just get going. I'm pretty hungry though. Have you eaten?"

"Not yet," I said.

"Tell you what—if you go to the store, I'll pay for everything, and then we can have a feast—how's that sound?"

She reached into her leather pants and pulled out a wad of hundreds and peeled me off one.

"Just get whatever you think you can cook, okay," she said, slumping into the kitchen chair and flipping her hair like a high school girl would, exposing her white face and newly polished fangs. "Keep whatever's left over for yourself. I know we've been eating a bunch of your food. Okay?"

Figured why not—I knew I could shop for good stuff for once and pocket some of the cash to send home. Passed Kurt, who was bouncing up the stairs with his fists tightly clenched. His smile was wide.

Outside, up the street, to the market out on Fillmore. Rows of Victorian houses gave way to projects very quickly and a row of streets that never appeared at all in a postcard.

There were dark blue vans with tinted windows outside of the projects that were very out of place from the scene I was used to. Men and women wearing those damn black polo shirts were walking around talking to everyone they could stop on the street. Groups of people gathered around them reading brochures. Must have been looking pretty run-down myself because one of them noticed me and slow-rolled his way to me.

"Hey—you don't have to rush away," he said. "We're just passing out a little bit of information is all. Need some people to be in a group for a few hours—no big deal. We pay cash. Interested?"

"I have a job already," I told him. "Besides, I'm not big on people in vans offering money. Not sure how you're getting people listen to you. Who the hell are you people, anyway?"

"Just trying to do a little good." He smiled. "Diabetes is a big problem in low-income communities. We represent some people who are hoping to be part of the cure. That doesn't interest you?"

He could see I wasn't buying it, and there was no use in pushing when he had others who were ready to sign their names to anything that would promise a dollar. Needed loot as much as anyone, but I always kept my mind on the long money. That short stack would leave you looking like a chump.

"Well, if you change your mind, give me a call," he sighed. "Doesn't have to be all business, either, if you catch me." He handed me some high-glossed card and walked away. If there was a trash can near me I would have tossed it, but I put it in my pocket and continued on with my shopping.

Walking to the store, I noticed more vans and more polo shirt people out there talking to folks from the neighborhood— collecting signatures and handing out cards.

Into the market and away from the people in vans.

Up and down the aisles of the market, not even looking at prices—buying cheeses, eggs, the nice coffee with the label, loaf of bread—everything I wanted. That's how you know if you have money: if you go to the market and don't check prices at all.

Walking back up the block, the polo shirt people were still collecting signatures and handing out phone numbers. Nobody was in any rush. Folks were lining up to talk to them.

Down Fillmore. Up McAllister again. Struggling with the weight of everything I'd bought. Consumption. Going back upstairs, Victor, the tweaker techno DJ from downstairs, poked his head through his door.

"What you getting into?" he blurted out. "Did you sign up for those studies? They're paying three hundred a pop if you go through the whole thing. That's cash."

"Not letting anyone test me out," I told him. "About to cook a feast. A good meal might make you see a little clearer. Want to join?"

"Food? No—I'm good. I'm good."

He slammed the door and went back inside.

My roommates were all sitting at the kitchen table, very relaxed and listening to my A Tribe Called Quest CD (the first one, which was already old at that point). They were bopping their heads and seemed to be into the music.

"Why don't I cook," I told them.

The kitchen was giant, so I had plenty of room to spread out what I'd just bought. Chopped, buttered, and laid it all down. The fresh basil and garlic I had bought as the base of the eggs started to fill the house.

Presented all of them with their plates, put the toast in the middle of the table, and hit the replay button on the CD. Must have been hungrier than all of them because I was devouring my meal, while they all ate slowly and stared in different directions. Now, I didn't grow up with a big family, so sitting at a table with a big group of people was fun for me—it was like in the movies, where everyone shares their stories and sets up their day.

Valerie turned to me and smiled, revealing a piece of basil on her fangs. "Thank you so much for doing this. We made the right choice."

Kurt was a little more loopy than the others. He was holding a card in his hand that I noticed to be exactly like the one that the polo shirt man outside had handed me.

"Where'd you get that?" I asked. "You're not thinking about going in there, are you?"

"This guy saw me looking out the window and called me down," he said, waving the card. "Thought he was asking me for a date, but turns out he wanted me to come in and take all these tests. Trying out some new medicine or something like that. Now, if you'd reconsider being our whip girl, I wouldn't have to think about things like that."

Almost out of there, though I couldn't show it.

CHAPTER 6

i.

Payday. Finally. Was pretty excited. Had my eye on a few places and different parts of town—anywhere but living with them was going to do me well. Knew that I wanted to live somewhere in the Mission because it was far enough away from everything but still just a jump above Market Street to be inside the city again.

Took the bus over the steep hills of Fillmore all the way down to the Marina.

Wearing the same outfit for days. Everything of mine was vanishing. They sold it all and wore what they couldn't sell. Junkies are not people you want to save or observe—you should get away as fast as possible before watching someone cooking up in a spoon starts to become as normal as lighting up a cigarette.

Every time I went to eat a bowl of cereal in the house, the bottom of the spoon was burnt black.

Made my way into the office of the chimney sweep sales team, and everyone was looking pretty sad.

"It's payday, people. What's up with the faces?" I asked.

One of the girls who worked the phone—a strong-faced girl from Oakland who always seemed to be tearing through a giant book and talking about school and what was ahead for her— looked at me and shook her head.

"Not going to pay us today," she said. "'Cash light,' he says, should have it next week. Don't worry about it—he does this all the time."

She went back to making calls. The other two people in there did the same, unconcerned with the lack of envelopes filled with cash waiting for them. Not me. My skin was about to be over-taken by the blood flying to its surface. Heard my pops coughing. Saw the goat-faced boy chomping on my cereal. Darren D. was playing with the toy at the bottom of the box.

"Where is he?" I yelled. "Out on a call?"

"Nope," peeped the crew-cut kid who never did anything beyond what he was told. "He's down the street at Uncle's."

That's all I needed to hear. Uncle's was a giant sports bar with girls wearing tight-fitting football shirts and short skirts with long tube socks. Opened the saloon-style doors and saw him, wearing half of his hobo costume, hunched over the bar and rub-bing the side of an almost empty beer glass. He noticed me but didn't pay any attention.

Didn't move at all.

"Where's my money?!" I yelled, causing most of the girls to turn their heads. "You need to pay me!"

The chimney sweep didn't move—just slowly sipped the end of his beer. Walked up to him slowly with the intention of ripping his head off if he didn't pay me. The lack of money in my pocket reminded me of a period in my childhood when we were pretty broke and dug around for cash in order to eat something. Not ashamed of any of it. My parents put food on the table no doubt, and we never went hungry, but it cost them their lives to do it. So when it was time for me to earn, I made sure I did exactly that, and I always got paid. Always.

Stood over him like a loan shark coming to collect on a punk. The tube sock girls watched with the curiosity of something out of the ordinary happening at work.

"Everything's fine," he said, waving everyone away and ordering me a beer. "Sit down, please. Sit down."

"I'm not here to sit down and have a beer with you. I'm here for my money. All of it. Now."

"You know, in life—there are so many roads we all take. You never know how it's going to end up. I had a wife—there was a house, kids, everything you see in the movies was there—but that's gone now. I like you. More than the rest there. Everyone else in the sales room, they don't have what you have. How about we sit down and talk like friends? I've had a bad day."

There was an envelope next to him with what iooked like the return address of some lawyer.

"You think I want to sit down with you? I want my fucking money!"

"Money," he said flatly. "Everyone wants their money. There's more to life than that. How about we sit down and become friends?"

Bent close to his ear and made sure he felt my eyes burning into the side of his head. "Look here, asshole, you're to lay my cash down on the table right now or I'm going to get some people down here to make life unreal for you."

Of course, I had no people to do any such thing, but in that moment I made myself believe I did, which, if you're talking to a weak enough person, creates reality.

Stood back for a second and looked at him. The state of his almost-dressed-up persona gave the impression of a Depression-era grifter who'd just gotten caught. He looked sad and broken, but that wasn't my concern. He was a man, and men were not supposed to break like this—not at a sports bar. Not in the Marina District. Not with a painted-on stubble beard!

Upped my voice. "This guy right here! This guy is stealing from us. He won't pay what he owes. He's a fucking bum!"

Thought it would embarrass him or shower him with shame, but his mood didn't change one bit. He reached into his pocket and pulled out a wrinkled envelope full of cash and put it on the bar.

"Here, that's all I have. Take it."

Grabbed the envelope and opened it up, seeing that there was close to five hundred in there.

"Will you sit down and have a drink now?" he said, sounding like a man on the brink and in need of a friend. "You've got what you asked for."

"You better come up with the rest of this," I said, backing away. "This guy's a bum!" was my final yell before hitting the streets again. Didn't go back to the office or ever see that guy again.

Out of work and a little bit harder now. No more jobs like that. No more chimney sweeps. I was short fifteen hundred dollars, and my plan was falling apart.

Went to a payphone and dropped in the change I kept in my pocket to call my pops. Mom answered.

"Everything okay?" she asked. "You normally don't call at this time."

"Yeah, I'm good. Just needed to connect. Can I talk to Pops?"

"He's sleeping right now. On some new medication that's making him drowsy. Wrote me something in case you called, though. Now where did I put it?"

Waited for her to fumble around for the note, reading all of the "Hello My Name Is" stickers pasted on the phone booth.

"Mom, you there?"

"Yes—yes, here it is. It says: 'Sarah, you can't be stopped. Find your highest voice and follow that.'"

Just then, a recording of an operator came on and asked for more money, but I didn't need to hear anything else.

2.

Valerie was nodding next to me when Darren D. walked in trying to cap off his fix, which broke Val out of her state.

"I shoot in my ass these days because it's not too great to have tracks on your arms," she said. "When you're dancing, they don't like to see what keeps you up on stage. Hell, if I was sober, you think I could stand looking into those eyes sitting there wanting to reach through me?

"The whole vampire thing—it's a reach for immortality— whatever that means. It preserves you inside. Everyone thinks that it's the heroin that kills you, but that's not what does it. It's the not having it. It's the fall to sobriety. Your body needing and not getting everything that it wants. Everything that it deserves. I see all these people walking in and out of my life with their wives and kids at home, with their jobs and security in the bank, with… with everything. And you know what? It's never enough. For me, for us, heroin is actually enough. Who can say they have enough in their lives?

"Me and this guy over here—though he's not as much here at this moment, as you can see—we're good. I make enough dancing every night to fill our habit. That's the thing, right? If I average around four hundred each night, plus all the stuff we do on the side, we can support what we do. I bring in the money, and this guy over here, he pulls his weight in a different way.

"Kurt and Marcy, they're scraping by. They won't last another two years. Not too long from now, one of them is going to come out and ask for a bit of what we have left. That's living off the droppings of others and counting on something beyond your control. You do that, you do that, and you're at the mercy of what other people do. I won't be like that. Ever."

Darren D. stood up from his nod.

"Let's go upstairs and take some pictures," he said. "I'm in the mood to be creative."

The two of them grabbed hands and walked up the stairs and into the next minute of their lives.

The bedroom door opened next to the kitchen and Kurt walked in, hunched over, looking around until he found the spoon that Valerie had just used. He grabbed it and disappeared back from where he came.

He looked like a ghost already to me.

i.

Heard screaming coming from the upstairs bathroom. It came again. Then again. Couldn't get back to sleep. The wolf dog came running into my room and barked for something, followed by the goat-faced boy, who always seemed to be interested in what was up on my walls. Think he was scoping out what he could steal and either sell or wear.

The scream came again, and this time I could hear Daren D. behind it. Kurt shook his head no, as if telling me not to pay any attention. Valerie came in, putting on her earrings and getting herself ready for work.

"Don't worry about that, it's an abscess," she said to me. "Happens all the time. Well, not all the time, but it's part of it. Not the pretty part.

"You have to see these parts of life. I'd love to share with you sometime and see what kind of stuff you're getting at in those zines. I have a small following here. They seem to like it, as you saw at the show. I don't know where I find time to do everything I do. The guy—remember the guy I was telling you about, who we wanted to have here if you would have let him? The cleaning guy who likes a few smacks? Anyway, he wants to be an editor— break into the magazine world. Let me know if you're in need of his services—I'd have to supervise him of course, but I wouldn't mind. Anyway, off to work. See you tonight."

She flipped her hair, zipped up her boots, and disappeared from the doorway. The goat-faced boy laughed and lit up a menthol.

Darren D. came in the door before my record finished playing. His arm was bandaged.

"You guys want to come with me to walk the dog?"

"It's so bright out," Kurt said.

"That's my line," Darren D. replied, flipping down his sunglasses. "Come on, we could use the exercise."

Both of them were pretty much all bones, but they were equally obsessed with staying thin. Being a male prostitute at that time, for their clients at least, had a little different twist than you'd think: All of the people who were paying were already ripped and in decent shape. They wanted little skinny man-boys to play with.

Junk helped keep that figure.

We all hit the block of McAllister and walked the wolf dog up towards the park. Being outside with people you're used to being in certain surroundings with is strange. The new frame around them often exposes who they really are. Either that, or it gives you a good look at who you really are.

> *Take a look at yourself,*
> *take a look at yourself,*
> *take one good look*
> *take a look at yourself.*

> —GURU

Felt warm seeing a familiar figure walking his bike up towards us, his right shoulder weighed down by a messenger bag. Alberto. My eyes weren't as quick to recognize him at that point. He flopped down, weighed down but not overwhelmed.

"Just did my last delivery of the day," he said, cracking open his Dr. Brown's Cream Soda. "They keep laying people off, though—less of us to do the same job. Bike messengers are vanishing from need."

"Well, I need you, obviously," I said, trying to lighten to the mood and show him how much he just brightened up my moment. "Not many people out there who appear at just the right time."

"I was hoping maybe you'd come by Lina's," he said. "I've been playing more games of Madden than I really should in hopes of seeing you again."

Darren D. and Kurt weren't into making new friends, so they got up and started playing catch with the wolf dog. The two of us closed our bubble a little more.

"I'm looking for a place and saving cash," I whispered to him. "The money part has been a grind, though. Nobody is hiring."

"Tell me about it," he replied, running his hand over his aching calf. "I'm going to have to find something new myself, and I can't do anything else other than this."

He looked over at my roommates talking with a couple of guys trying to strike up a deal.

"What are you going to do?" I asked.

He opened up his messenger bag and pulled out a small Day Keeper held together with duct tape.

"Did a delivery today. Bunch of floor plans to this place down south of Market Street. It was an old warehouse—but the guys there were turning it into some kind of office. They were pretty young—at first I thought they were painters or something, but turned out they owned the business. We got to talking a bit, and they told me to come on in for an interview—and to bring any of my friends who needed work with me."

"An office job?" I asked, slightly surprised. "What kind of work is it?"

"He didn't say. Just told me to come down and interview next Friday. Not sure I could go inside an office, but might not have a choice. Word is the messenger shop is closing."

"How could that be? Everyone needs documents delivered quickly. How are they going to replace you?"

He leaned back and smiled, but it was more condescending than happy. "You've been in your own world," he laughed. "Haven't you been paying attention to what's happing? Everyone's saying Internet. Where you been?"

"Trying to escape," I told him, looking at my roommates on the other side of the hill playing catch while trying to score.

Showed him the card the man from earlier had given me. "I was thinking of maybe going to these guys for some cash. Hate to do it, but might not have a choice."

Alberto almost choked on his soda and shot up with a mood change from beyond himself. "Who the hell gave you that? Are they still around?"

"I don't think so," I said. "Didn't see them when we left the house. Said they were battling diabetes."

His face had gone rigid.

"Those are the guys from the drug companies," he said. "They're looking for people to experiment on. I tried to tell you before!"

"Your fliers. Right."

"Don't be light with it," he fumed. "I saw some of their vans downtown trying to talk to people on the unemployment lines. They follow the layoffs. You should pay closer attention to what's happening around you."

"Don't I? You don't know much beyond your own agenda," I blurted out, not realizing I was crying. "You know my pops is at home trying to save his life with these kind of tests. What the hell do you know? Where the hell is someone supposed to turn?"

Was bawling, and pissed off that I was. Alberto unclenched his face.

"Come on," he said, standing up and extending his hand to help me up. He was set against the sun, where I couldn't see anything but the light behind him. "I'm taking you to get something to eat."

He pulled me up, and we walked down to the sidewalk, where he balanced his bike enough for me to climb on the handlebars and rolled me away from the very people I was trying to escape from.

2.

We went down to the Mission to have a burrito at the spot on Sixteenth and Guerrero.

He saw me notice his wrists taped up when he took the foil-wrapped burritos from the man behind the counter.

"MUNI didn't see me," he said, taking a sip of his horchata. "Nothing broken—but sprains add up. My family are fast healers. Don't worry."

"What makes you think I'm worried about you?" I asked. "You're so serious all the time. Believe me, I've got tons on my shoulders—as much as most and more than some—but I don't walk around with this pissed-off look all the time."

"You didn't give those guys in the van your information, did you?" he asked, trying to change the subject.

"What do you got against them?"

"You never read that flyer?"

"Did you read my zine?"

"Every word. Twice."

We walked out the door and headed over to Dolores Park and sat in between the herb sellers on the flat part of the park, with the families up top who mixed dog-watching with baby-playing.

"You've got some amazing talent," he said to me. "What are you doing wasting it with these bullshit jobs? The way you take what most people throw away and turn it to gold—you show people what they're supposed to be looking at. Not many people can put it all together."

"What's so special about that?" I asked. "It's what I've always done. Nothing special. Just me. Everyone has something that's just them. Wouldn't mind if someone noticed, though."

"I notice everything you do," he said, not moving his eyes from mine, then shifting a bit when I didn't return the same intensity. "If we could make more than a few of these, others might too. Speaking of getting noticed—did you read my flyer?"

Pulled my hair back behind my ears, which was just long enough to stay and clip over. "No," I said, "but that doesn't mean what you have on there isn't worth reading. Let me see."

He handed it to me. Read like this:

> *The drugs you are taking are not curing you. They don't want you cured. You being sick is keeping them in business. They are creating these diseases: acid reflux, sleep-work syndrome, depression, and many others. They want you to go and ask your doctor if they have anything to help with the symptoms of these diseases.*
>
> *Doctors are being paid thousands of dollars to prescribe these drugs to you. The medical industry is collapsing and forcing them to turn to the drug companies to stay afloat.*

If you are not sick, if you don't believe you are sick, they can't make money. Each ad you see is going to tell you to "Ask Your Doctor" for a specific medication to help cure you of these symptoms. They are going to have you ask by name. There is nothing there for you. Read the labels. The small print. Everything is designed to make you even sicker. They are selling you death.

Put the flyer down and looked into Alberto's eyes. Needed to see what was inside of him.

"Why is this so important to you?" I asked. "I mean, is this a crusade with a heart, or are you just fighting to fight because you're losing everything?"

"You—that's right at me. Some stuff I've put down so it wouldn't come up. You need all of that to help me?"

"If you want me in this battle—and I mean really in—you're going to have to let me inside of you. It's the only way it'll work."

He sat back and looked at me for a long minute.

"My big sister—I love her so. When her friends would come over from school, they'd all get high in back of the apartment and then come up to our room. We shared because it was a one bedroom. They were stoned out of their minds. I was about twelve—they were all seventeen. They'd take turns practicing kissing on me. Was amazing. She'd laugh hysterically because I had no idea what I was doing. They'd all leave and we'd go out to Nations for some burgers.

"She could eat pretty much anything she wanted because she ran cross-country. Was on her way to a scholarship at UCLA. She kept telling me we'd be surfing together.

"Every guy was after her, but she was in love with this one guy, and only this one guy. They were each other's first love. They planned out their whole lives together.

"As young couples do when they start dating, they started having sex wherever they could, so she decided to go on birth control so they didn't have to have condoms at each moment. She wasn't about to give up her dreams and get pregnant. Since they were only sleeping with each other, she didn't see the harm in it.

"Just before she graduated, with her scholarship locked up, she was running her last cross-country race when, running through Golden Gate Park, the left side of her body went numb. She collapsed. She was paralyzed forever on that side of her body. The guy, who she thought would stay with her forever, left after trying to deal with it. Can't say I don't understand—no way a teenager can handle all of that.

"Turns out that the stroke was a reaction from the birth control. It said so right on the box, only the letters are so small you can't really see.

"Obviously, they pulled the scholarship, so she still lives in that same apartment with my mother. So, I guess, there's your reason behind the fight."

He looked at me deep, but there wasn't a hint of a tear. That had all taken place, and now he was all about action. Figured that, in return, I could return to emotion instead of the sympathy.

"You're saying the right things," I told him, putting my hand on his sprained wrist. "Just in the wrong way. Nobody wants to be told the truth straight like that. You need to hide it a little, wrap it in a story to entertain them a bit. The days of the soapbox preacher are over. Revolutions, if you want them, need to be subversive."

"With the information I have," he said, stretching out his knee, which let out a pop, "and the ability you have to make it golden, we just might make something memorable."

"Came here to do something amazing," I told him. "Maybe this, somehow, is part of it. Can't see how it's going to make me any money, but something feels right about it. Sometimes just have to go with that feeling."

CHAPTER 8

i.

Excited about getting some work done with Alberto, but needed a new roommate back at the house, and even though inside I knew I was leaving, the immediate wouldn't leave me alone.

When I saw *her*, all of that crashed around me. She had dark skin and these amazing blue eyes with lips that I wanted to lock around. There was a slight discoloration on her forehead, but it only added to her. The girl she was going to share the room with stood behind her friend and didn't make eye contact when she spoke.

You know when you're in love because every piece of your body betrays you. With Alberto, it was like the love of a good novel—something that could alter your life path—but with her, everything reached inside of me.

She moved like a child who was struggling to carry a woman's body. They had just talked to the vampires and the goat-faced boy and seemed charmed enough by how unusual they were. The mix of that and the amazing house usually drew people in who were in the middle of a search for the unique.

"Is it fun living here?" she asked me, tilting her head down slightly—revealing her age, but not too much. "I'm Josephine, and this is Kerri. Thing is, I'm a cat and she's a butterfly, so you'll need to know that. To me, this girl right here is my center for beauty in the world. Can you see that?"

Just as she said it, I noticed the amazing eyelashes on Kerri and saw the butterfly. Not all peace-faced like that normally, so it was kind of a big deal for me to see. When you fall for someone, they start pointing out things and events in the world that you don't normally realize, causing you to believe they are opening it up for you. When Josephine spoke, she let the last note of each word just hang in the air by clicking her tongue just enough on the roof of her mouth.

They moved in, and I helped bring all of their stuff up the first flight of stairs. Did my best to walk behind Josephine. She caught me but liked that I was bold enough to do it. Sat in the room while they unpacked to see what kind of life they were bringing out of their boxes.

Now Kerri, she and Darren D. got along right away. That dude was wearing one of his Underoos that day—might have been a Tweety Bird, I don't know. He freaked because she had all of these coloring books and a collection of Crayola crayons, including a little factory that allowed you to make your own colors out of the nubs that couldn't be used anymore. He told her about his My Little Pony collection, and she went wild. There was this sewing machine in the last box she unpacked, and she promised to make little night quilts for each of the ponies.

Kerri sported rubber bracelets of colors that didn't match. Josephine wore pretty much all black and had only a few boxes of stuff. No books. None. She had a box of CDs—mostly the Smiths, Morrissey, and some Depeche Mode—you know, things you should run away from if you ever see a girl you're falling in love with pull out of a box.

They decorated their room quick—Kerri doing most of the work and Josephine commenting about how much she loved everything. They talked about how they would make Shrinky

Dinks that would go around the edges of the room. Kurt liked that and got excited to have a Shrinky Dink party—went ultimate goat on that one.

The only thing Josephine decorated her part of the room with was a picture of this boy—he was young in the picture, but looked like he was about to take a journey. Had a beard, a backpack, and a baseball hat that seemed awkward on him. She put that up right next to her bed and held her stare on it for an uncomfortable amount of time. Kerri put up a poster of some Care Bears. A small tear held up in the bottom of Josephine's bottom eyelid. Kerri looked at me, kind of shaking her head without shaking her head.

Everything was unpacked.

2.

The two girls in the house made everything a little lighter for all of us. My attraction to Josephine put a slow roll on my plans to move.

Would visit Alberto in the day and get the reports, interoffice memos, and countless lab results he had stockpiled through the years. He made sure his messenger route was on that of anyone who dealt with the pharmacy companies—accounting, PR, lab results, and, of course, the advertising companies.

At night, I'd get to work on the *Luddite* issues that started attacking the drug companies. My gift to him for trying to be a great man was to make him a zine out of everything he had been fighting for.

Colin would meet me at Kinko's in the Sunset District by SFSU, the school I was supposed to go to. Would always see kids printing out their papers at the last minute of late-night panic.

He'd do his comic strip and help me out when he saw me struggling, trying to draw. Invited Nick as well and could have used him, as getting known was what he was all about, but he vanished into the club scene and faded out of my life. Goes like that sometimes—without any notice, people leave.

Would bring home the completed prototype of *Luddite*, along with the stack of papers that were going to become the zine after it got stapled just right down the spine. Kerri would stay up, but never until the sun came up, while Josephine had no problem making it all the way through.

Colin would go bombing by himself in the blank canvas of the city.

Josephine always had trouble going to sleep, which was nice for me because nobody else could stay up with her other than me.

After hours of collation, she'd crash and I'd watch her cheek get warmed by the sun that came through the tiny window in my bedroom.

3.

"This is good stuff," Alberto said over a lunch box I'd brought him and he interpreted the wrong way. He had the latest *Luddite* pressed open on the table on the other side of the box. "You took the labels of Gerber baby food and made them into coffins filled with money and pills. What does that even mean?"

"Who cares?" I told him. "People are going to read the article below it, talking about how in third world countries, parents are offering their babies for clinical trials on new medications because companies don't need to report what happens outside of the country. Twist and shout."

"When are you going to let me meet that team of yours?" he said, trying to hug me. "You all, especially you, are amazing."

"Isn't the time we spend together enough?" I asked him. "How come boys always want more, no matter what you give? Amazing to me."

Felt bad about the stinger to him, but couldn't tell him that I didn't want him around Josephine. Was trying to find a way to stash her in a pocket somewhere and bring her with me into the world I was trying to escape into.

"It's not that I want more—it's, well, yes, I guess I do want more. Nothing wrong with that—with trying to be part of something."

"The only thing I'll ever be part of is my family, and those who become my family," I told him. "As for causes and movements, I don't mind contributing when I can—which is kind of what I'm doing with you—for you. But to have that responsibility of being the leader—no. What I could use now is some cash."

"I understand that," he said. "Usually the only people who say money isn't important are those who have it."

He paused and looked out of the park. Something in his face changed.

"That card that Valerie gave you," he said. "You still have it?"

"I think so. Why?"

"Well," he started in, "we might be able to take care of everything with one swoop. Get your dad the money he needs and get us the info we need to really expose those assholes. Right now we're on the surface—this can be our chance to dig in."

"You want me to go work for them!" I yelled, then pulled myself back a bit. "You've lost your mind for sure."

Then I thought about what he was saying.

"Well, maybe you haven't lost your mind—but you're asking a lot."

He leaned back and smiled. "The information you'll get from them will make *Luddite* legendary. That might not mean short money, but in the long run—it might bring you more than any job you might take. This could be the base of it all."

That was the thing about Alberto—when he had a vision about something happening, he let himself be taken away completely with it. You couldn't help but get into that scope of how he saw the world—it was so amazing because he believed his plans were actually going to change life for the better. Why the hell not? Make my money, make my art, make my contribution. The man was offering me everything I came to San Francisco for. It just wasn't how I thought it was going to look like, but it never is.

"You wouldn't be joining them," he said. "It would be a fight from the inside. That's what the CIA and other organizations did for years to erode any type of revolutions that took place in this country. They had a plant on the inside. Think of how close you can get."

"I need to think on it," I said, grabbing my stack of *Luddite* to put in Laundromats, cafés, and anywhere else people might have been waiting around. "That's climbing right into their belly. Though I have to say, the chance to build on this—to get *Luddite* into the hands of more people—that's enticing. It's appealing. How much money do you think?"

"Six figures is not unheard of, but high seventies to start. Unlimited as you move up. These people have money to burn. They're passing billions to each other. What you make in the office is going to be crumbs, but those crumbs can feed a whole lot of—"

He stopped short.

"Rats," I said. "You were about to call me a rat."

"All of us are," he said. "Just running around scrambling for these crumbs they're laying out there for us, but some are getting bigger pieces than others. Each job, it's just a shake from the big bag. We kill each other just to hold a crumb for a second, but it's not enough to sustain you. They want you battling each other for it."

"Why don't *you* go inside, then?" I asked. "You know exactly what to look for. They want people like you anyway in there. All tatted up and jaded. You'd be like Jesus."

We both busted up laughing and took a few bites of burritos before speaking again.

"I tried to be in an office once," he said. "Just a bunch of mass confusion being spread. I couldn't take hiding how I felt. First chance I smelled any bullshit I'd just yell it out full blast at them.

"Wouldn't last a day. Didn't when I tried in the past. That's why messengering was perfect. They handed me these documents outlining plans on how to sell poison and call it medicine. They never paid any attention to me. Getting my hands on all of that inside information is impossible now. They aren't handing it over to me anymore."

Took a step back to look at him to feel everything he was saying. Could see how it would make things easier for me and better for him. Figured I'd have to scrounge for cash anyway, so why not make the big money, send it home, and really get my work out to the people I wanted to see it—finally the ability to live above ground but still exist underground. Wanted to say yes right there. True, I trusted Alberto more than anyone at that point, but I had to hold my emotions inside. Always kept in practice with that.

"Let me think on it," I said. "I'll let you know in a few days. Have to roll out now anyhow."

"Where you going?"

"Just going," I answered. "Just going."

4.

Josephine had drifted to sleep in my lap. Was six a.m. and was just putting issues of *Luddite #6: The Adverse Events Issue* together for release. The cover showed a cartoon of mice being let out of jail, while homeless people were being marched in. Alberto had been collecting documents about how pharmaceutical companies were using homeless people in the city to run experiments in early clinical trials after the FDA had said that testing on mice was no longer a viable option for release on humans. Rather than go overseas and work on starving people who'd sell their youngest child to help feed their other two, it was much cheaper to work on an expendable local population everyone wanted to go away anyhow.

They set up a dummy business, a call center, hired all of these homeless people, spent the next six months injecting them with early-stage tests of prefilled syringes, and watched how it affected them throughout the day.

The called it a sleep/work study because they were able to watch their subjects at night and during the day. Heavy stuff, but the copies of documents that Alberto had stockpiled over the years made for amazing stories that our readership just ate up. Everyone liked reading about conspiracies and evil corporations. Guess when people hear about it, they somehow think they're contributing to the solution.

Josephine rolled over in my lap trying to get comfortable, but woke herself up with a jolt.

"Just a bad dream," she said, lying back down. "Well, I wish it was a dream. I wake up each day wishing it was a dream." She looked at the picture of the boy looking like he was going somewhere.

I didn't want to know the history there—I felt its darkness and pain—but I put on the radio that always played good jazz into the early mornings and asked if she wanted to tell me who the boy was.

"Him?" she asked, finally lighting up. "That's the one I killed. Well, I didn't kill him with my hands, but my mouth and the words that came out of it—I did.

"See, we were in love before I left for San Francisco. I was about to go off to college, and he was older in years and in spirit. I told him he needed to go to Europe and have sex with as many people as he could so he wouldn't take the physical part of love so seriously. He always did that. It's not too serious, you know.

"Anyhow, he said he'd go, but he wouldn't be with anyone but me—that I was the only place he wanted to move inside of. Such a boy, but I loved him so. He was a genius and very much enjoyed being one. I knew, though, that if we stayed together, I'd crush him, so before he went away, I slept with a few people and let him know about it. I thought it would free him. He took it pretty well—I thought he did, at least.

"The morning he was supposed to leave, he showed up at my house after not talking to me for a few days. I could feel him slipping away from me, but I loved him so much—I wanted to let that happen. I wanted to feel that pain for him. It was a pleasure for me to take that away, to give him the power of being the one who left.

"This picture, I took it of him the day he was supposed to go. Look at his face, how beautiful it was. It is.

"He handed me a mix tape—said to listen to it for the next few hours while his plane took off. It was all of the songs and people he taught me how to go inside of. Some of them might be corny I guess, but when you love somebody all of that trite thought leaves and you just enjoy what is. He kissed me and walked out the door.

"I spent the afternoon laying on my bed wearing nothing but his Specials T-shirt and listening to his music play. I thought of him moving through the sky into great experiences.

"I was listening to 'Sailing' by Christopher Cross when my door opened. My mother never opened the door without knocking. She looked petrified to speak to me. I had a huge smile on my face, though, because I didn't care about anything other than the fact that I had sent him on his way out into the world. Then I got the news. He hadn't gone on his trip at all. He took himself out to the ocean—the place where we first made love, actually—and drowned himself by walking in, weighed down by the backpack he was supposed to go to Europe with.

"He had me listening to the music as his funeral march. He was so smart, even when he was being cruel. He was."

Looked at her face that had cried so much about that constant memory that any ability to shed a tear had evaporated.

The music played somberly, and we both let it be. Thought of my pops right there and what he would have said to Josephine to get her head right. She enjoyed the blues, though, and San Francisco was as good as any city to feel that way.

"How about we go out?" I said, just before the sunrise. "I'll take you to North Beach and show you how I see the city."

"I'd like that," she told me, putting her head back in my lap, then looking up past me to the ceiling. "It's good to see the world like others want to."

5.

Knew I could save her if she let me, and even if she didn't, I would still try to be the one to bring her out of the darkness she'd created. My pops I could save with money, but Josephine it had to be with love—whatever that word meant.

She had asked if I knew where to get some speed, and I told her of course, though I had never tried the stuff. Other than smoking herb once in a while and that crazy trip on the beach with Alberto, I had lived a pretty sober existence.

What was I going to do—was trying to get a girl. Went downstairs to Victor's and asked if he could get any. He smiled. He was a nervous guy but didn't shake. Was sure he never slept. There were no pictures on his wall, and he had only a simple couch that made the absence of everything else even more noticeable.

Turntables were set up on the back wall, and he usually wore a pair of headphones around his neck. The records he put down just played—could never tell what his role in the whole thing was. He never DJed at any clubs, only talked about what others were doing. Strange guy but nice in his own kind of way. He was patient and never in a rush to get anywhere or do anything. Though everyone I had lived with had been there for some time, each one told me that Victor was there when they all moved in.

He made a quick phone call, and within a few minutes there was a knock on the door. A kid came in—tall and skinny with a baseball hat tacoed out.

A few words to each other and it was done. Door closed behind him. Smile on Victor's face.

"Just a line, is that cool?" he asked.

"Sure," I said, though a little worried that he would take too much and there wouldn't be enough for Josephine. That's the "carrying charges" you have to pay when dealing with too many middlemen. From what he told me, this was pretty good stuff. Glass. They looked like little shards broken up into tiny pieces. He poured himself out what looked to be a healthy amount and started chopping with his food stamp card until it was as fine as it could get. Took out an already trimmed straw that was under his turntable. Inhaled.

"You know," he said, "we could split this bag if you like. I totally don't mind going half with you."

"If there's any left over after our date, I'll roll down and sell you what's left."

"There's not going to be anything left, chica," he said, smiling. "I know that girl. She's gonna eat it all. It's her style to do so. Careful of that."

He handed me the bag, I gave him the cash, he put on his headphones and started listening. Stood in silence for a minute before realizing he was in his own world and there was no need for a proper goodbye.

Back upstairs. Passed Valerie as she was on her way to work—hair wet and eyes wild. Could see her fangs because she was yelling back up to Darren D. to make sure to clean up the room tonight. A cab honked from downstairs, and she bolted away, taking out her compact to start covering up.

6.

Wore a just-above-the-knees skirt with my black Chucks and socks that went above my ankles but dropped over them just a bit. Went back and forth over the top, but settled on small white tee and a cardigan sweater that buttoned from the top. Josephine wore a black T-shirt with black pants.

There is a church in the center of Washington Park—it's the place where Joe DiMaggio and Marilyn Monroe got married. Gorgeous structure that attracts tourists, shelters locals with a place to kneel and pray, provides schools, and gives off a magnificent backdrop on rare sunny days with blue skies and a large patch of grass to lay out on.

Always one to try to make a production out of things, I thought it'd be a great idea to do a nice line of speed while kneeling down to pray in front of the Virgin Mary inside the church. That was my plan—my shot at being remembered and starting the relationship off right. Mind you, I already knew that her ex-boyfriend had killed himself because of her and that she was haunted by that, but I was thinking about how to be remembered. Fantastic.

Went down to get her in her room and found her lying in her bed watching Kerri draw.

"You ready?" I asked, thinking that perhaps she'd notice me and melt away just a bit.

"You sure you don't need me to stick around?" she asked Kerri, grabbing her bag. "You should come with us. She's taking me to North Beach. You should come. We're going to City Lights and doing—what else are we doing?"

She was smiling big and talking soft, like the world was being planned out for her.

Kerri shook her head no, but held her stare on me.

We walked out into the three p.m. sunshine. Both of our sunglasses covered each other. Not sure what bus we jumped on first, but I think it was the 22 Fillmore—that was going to take us all the way up, and we could walk down to North Beach from there.

She moved slow, cautious, as if she was afraid every step beneath her was going to crush a newly constructed sandcastle. It was the first time I'd seen her out in natural light. When she sat down in the bus, it was like being absorbed into the side of the metal frame. Kids drew on the ceilings and yelled loudly. They were looking at her, but she was lost through the window while I concentrated on her reflection.

We smiled and shared looks all the way until Van Ness met Broadway, then descended towards North Beach. Kept checking to see if the bag of speed was still in my pocket.

A breeze came off the bay. She breathed. Smiled.

"You know, I'm glad you came into my life," she told me, rocking back on her heels, then up onto her toes. "I needed somebody to talk with and to lead me a little. I've been playing that role for so long. You don't mind, do you? I trust you not to take advantage of that position."

"That's what I'm here for," I let her know. "Maybe we just needed to run into each other during this part of our lives."

Started planning our years together in San Francisco as we walked down the hill. Maybe I'd get my zine up and running into a full magazine after more people knew about it. Josephine could come and visit me when I was done with work, or I'd go and meet her when she was done with whatever it was that she wanted to do.

"What's your life look like in ten years?" I asked. "What do you want out of the world?"

She stopped for a moment, then picked up again. "I guess—I think something in forensics," she said. "I never minded tracing the root of why things happened. I think I'd be satisfied doing something like that. Looking over dead bodies to figure out what caused them to stop breathing."

Hmm. Not very romantic, I thought, but then was able to convince myself that the oddity of her chosen profession made her unique. We reached the tunnel that led into North Beach and walked through in silence on the railed-off edges, feeling the hot breezes made by the cars zooming by.

Emerged from the tunnel and saw the Big Al's Sex Shop sign. That's not the intro I wanted to give her to North Beach, so we hung a left and went through a back alleyway through

Chinatown, where the ducks hanging in the windows and the smells of fish didn't go with the picture I was trying to create, either.

Stick to the plan. To the church.

Up Grant and back onto Columbus. We had missed City Lights, which is the thing I had been telling her about and the place I wanted to show her, but it was of no matter. Later. We'd hit it later. The plan. Stick to the plan.

Up Columbus and without that wandering approach to it, with the determination of a place to get to, the wonders of the neighborhood faded away.

We got to the church and stood on the grass. All around us, everyone dipping in and out of moments. We walked in—not looking at any of the sculptures or paintings on the wall. Tried to usher her to the Virgin Mary as quick as I could, but she stopped to light a candle.

"Would you light one for him?" she asked. "I—It's just something that I need to do. Don't feel you need to be a part of this. It only haunts me."

Hundreds of candle flames moved back and forth, reflecting in the blackness of her pupils. If I lit the candle, did that mean I needed to abandon the plan? Lit the candle and felt her touch my forearm. The feeling of that touch, though—she was trying to reach out to him. Had to battle his ghosts and take away anything that might have been accomplished in the church. Of course, this wasn't part of my initial plan. Just wanted to create a moment for us to put in a frame. The circumstances of everything that was happening around me made me believe it was fate—that what I was about to do was proper.

Reached into my pocket and showed her the pack of crystals. She smiled, but it wasn't happy—a mask of skin moved over her, not making her any less beautiful, but certainly less accessible.

Didn't matter. She was an image for me that I was filling in. We knelt down, and I poured two nice lines out on a credit card. She took hers down without a problem. Went next, though not really knowing what I was doing. Needed to break it into two separate lines. She lifted her head up as if a prayer had just been completed while I was coughing and gagging. The priest even came over to me and offered a cup of water.

Josephine smiled. "What's next?"

Lifted my head and saw the statue in front of me and knew it was time to get out of there and on with the rest of our date. As we walked outside of the church, she grabbed my hand and whispered so close to my ear that the inner arch of her lip rubbed against my lobe.

"I need friends right now, okay?"

She touched me. That's all I knew. Heart shooting through my rib cage. Hands shaking. Needed hers to calm me down. Where was the next stop on the date? Sun was gone but it wasn't night. Bottom of my teeth felt smooth. That helped. Held her tight and kissed her. She didn't refuse but didn't give in. The anticipation was over and action had taken center stage.

We started out just like that.

"What do you want to do?" I asked her. "We can do anything."

"I thought you had everything planned," she said. "What about City Lights?"

Yes. Yes. City Lights. Exactly. Grabbed her hand and we rushed back down Columbus towards City Lights Bookstore. The evening crowd was coming in. All dressed up. Prices in the restaurants were changing from lunch to dinner. Led her towards the bookstore and tried to shield her from all the people I didn't want her to see. Where were all the locals? Where were the meats and cheeses hanging from the windows? Only saw BMWs. Pieces of conversations echoed in my ears.

"We're getting things beyond cheap—I'm telling you, now's the time to buy."

"Don't worry about what you're with on the weekends—you're not going to marry it, are you?"

"I'm bored with everywhere I've eaten."

That strip of street stayed in my head, but I was trying to get us to the bookstore that gripped onto the past for me. We made it inside. Shaking. She was doing what I was doing and looking where I told her to look and listening to what I was telling her to listen to, but nothing was as it was. The music was this furious tune that made my eyes rattle like the last bounces of a plinko ride. The man who was usually behind the counter with the mellow cat must have been off that night. A girl leaning so she'd be noticed leaning purposely paid no attention to us.

Upstairs? They had built a new poetry section.

"Listen, listen to the sounds of the steps!" I shouted quickly while sweating out what was left of the day. "Isn't that sound amazing? History? Yes? Can you feel it?"

She nodded but not how I wanted her to. The pocket book series of books. Ginsberg. *Howl.* Save me. It didn't. The sentences ran over each other and burned me inside. Disgracing my church now. Served me right. Bought her a copy anyway so she'd have something to remember the experience with and had both of us sign it.

Outside. Night. No calming down. Took a joint out of my pocket to calm me down, and passed it to her once I had taken a puff. She passed.

"I don't smoke," she said. "Messes with my head."

"Don't these crystals do that to you?"

"No. For me, it just speeds up life to the end, which is where I'm headed anyway. Besides, it kind of calms me down so I can focus on the now. Don't worry though, we're going to have some fun from here on out. Smoke that up, I think it will calm you down. There was a lot pressure on you tonight. You did everything you wanted, right?"

"I wanted to show it all to you."

"You did. I can see that. We're good now."

She grabbed me and pulled me into the alley of City Lights, and we made out under the giant airbrushed head of Edgar Allen Poe.

My first ever girlfriend.

CHAPTER 9

i.

It roasted in July—a year in the city now. Downtown at the bike messengers' wall, waiting with Alberto Orca for a call to come in over his radio. The newspaper he was reading had a headline that read, "Electronic Mail: The End of Human Delivery?"

Watched for a long minute to take a full mental snapshot, which I'd later tell Colin, who did an amazing cover for the *End of Analog* issue of *Luddite*. So sublime: a bike leaned up against a repair shop with an eviction notice taped to the door.

"The calls are coming less and less," he said. "They just laid off a third of the company."

"How else are architects and designers—even lawyers and accountants—how else are they going to deliver the giant stacks of papers? They'll need you forever. The city is lost without you. You're its veins."

Alberto drank from his giant cup of coffee and didn't flinch when his radio came on, sending him for his next pickup.

"We're not gone today, at least," he said, finishing his coffee. "Have you thought about what we talked about? Going inside and exposing them?"

"Yeah—I have. The money would help set my pops up, my moms too—and the zines that would come out of it could be revolutionary in a way that satisfies both of us. You for effect and me for exposure. I'm ready."

"That's what I wanted to hear," he said, adjusting the band on his glasses. "It's time we combine our interests. No doubt you'll be out of that crazy house you're in."

My mood changed slightly, and he noticed. I think people notice subtle movements when they're so into you.

"Not yet," I told him. "Don't have the money to move, and—" I couldn't tell him about Josephine. Didn't really want to tell anyone about her, not until I saved her, at least.

"Well, we got to get you out of there," he said. "You're free to come crash at my place—just until you can get going."

"That might work," I said, looking away so he didn't see what I was really thinking, then changing the subject. "Been a while since I talked to my pops. He doesn't come to the phone these days. Mom does most of the talking and just tells me that they're short on cash, that he believes in me, and that at some point, I'm going to figure out what to do with my life."

"No pressure though," Alberto said, mounting his bike and laughing as much as he could. "We'll prep on how you're going to interview later on. Don't worry about things too much. There's a reason all of this is happening."

He pedaled down Market Street into the fog, mixing with the stream of MUNI trains and banged-up cars.

2.

Got home to find a movie crew in the house. Cameras and cords were strung everywhere. False lighting was coming from upstairs. Downstairs, Kurt and his woman stayed behind their doors, which I later found out they were bribed to do with a day and a half's worth of junk. Went upstairs to relax and wait for Josephine to come home, only to find Valerie being made up to look as vamp as possible. The letters on the side of the cameras read HBO. She seemed comfortable inside of the whole affair. Darren D. stood with his arms crossed over themselves, having been told more than a few times to stay out of the shot.

The director looked at the shot he was about to create and waited for her to come into frame. Valerie was concentrating on the regular spiral notebook that she was holding. She flipped up her hair and did what she could to ignore the makeup they had put on her.

She came into frame and read.

"I have seen what you all look like on the other side of the mirror. The locked doors have no meaning for me. I am your lunch break—did you bring me some takeout to eat while you held your cock or had me pull on your skin until you bleed? I see that in you, and because you made me see that inside of you. I see it inside of everyone. So many of you have asked—*on your lunch breaks*, on your way home to your families, on your business trips—just to have me hurt you in some, how do you all call it, 'exotic way.' It's just another job to do.

"You think I'm afraid of the sun or pretty things, or that all of it needs to be black? That there is some depression behind me? The image you see in front of you is something that you've created. I look like what you want me to be. If it weren't for you, I might survive in some other way for a living, but since you want to throw your money at me, since you want to pay me to be this way, to tie you up and make you drink your own blood, to beat you while you kneel down in front me, I will be that. I am, after all, only your employee. I only get paid if the client is happy.

"How is my presentation so far? I'll tell you a story now, in the middle of all of this, just so you can be removed. There was a girl who came to strip at the club. She was already gone. This isn't a tale of someone fresh off the bus, understand. She was on her way down, anyway. That's a big difference between them and me, understand. See, I chose this because I knew of people like you. This girl—we'll call her Simmer—she chose this *because* of people like you. There was too much touching from the wrong hands at some point, and she hit the road to do this.

"When Simmer got to us, we took her in like a family member—as much of a family as we were. We tried to keep the owner away and made sure if she did anything physical with the customers, that they were the tame ones. Nobody wanted anything to do with pushing her over the edge. We'd rather keep her on it for as long as possible. Not sure if that's good or bad, but it just is. Right.

"So one day, it was slow, and we just all kind of got behind her and held her. I wanted to make her feel better. She'd go into fits of crying about the same stuff that all you probably cry about. Money. Boys. Life. Past. All of it just welled up in her. I didn't give her any heroin because it's not an answer for that.

"Simmer waited for us to go onstage and grabbed my purse. She shot herself up but had no idea what she was doing—then passed out and that was that. Before we called the police, everyone hid their works and everything else inside the space behind the mirrors in the dressing rooms. Yes, there is always a secret compartment. I didn't feel bad that it was my needle that killed her. I still have it, as a matter of fact. It has one of her last drops of blood in it. For me, that's kind of pure and fascinating. Something I would never be able to buy from a store. Something that nobody would be able to buy for me. It's something that I could do and fetch for myself. Self-indulgence and satisfaction are really the things that keep me going.

"I can't say that I was sad about Simmer dying, but I was bothered with my involvement in it."

She closed her notebook and went over to Darren D., who hugged her tight. Both of them were in tears. The entire crew was silent, and the director wanted to keep the film rolling. Darren D. went into the bedroom with Valerie, and the crew followed. They took some stock footage of the My Little Pony collection to run when Valerie was talking about the trophy case.

On the monitors set up in the ballroom, I could see Valerie take out her strap-on, adjust it, and bend Darren D. over. She went to work hammering him while crying at the words she had just written. He smiled and shouted at the same time, exposing his fangs and looking like a puppy dog finally being taken on a long walk after waiting at home all day.

I'd had enough. This was my everyday. I went into my room, shut my door, put on a record as loud as it would play, and wondered where I was in life.

CHAPTER 10

i.

Went to go and meet Alberto after work to talk about what to say on the interview, and found him pleading with his dispatcher.

"We're closing it down," Frank the dispatcher said. "It's just not going to work. End of the month, though. I could keep everyone 'til then."

"I'll buy it," Alberto said without thinking. "No need to close it down."

"You don't have enough to do that, son," Frank responded in between bites of his sandwich. "'Sides, even if you did, I wouldn't sell it to you. You can't make money doing this anymore. In a few years, we'll be a novelty act. There's just not a need anymore. Look at these beautiful banged-up beasts—hell, look at the bruises on your own body. You look like a damn leopard with all those spots! You're smart, though. You should be making real money out there. Won't be too hard for you."

"I chose this, though, Frank. Never felt right doing anything else. How am I going to keep from moving all day long?"

"Well, I'll tell you this. Good thing you live in a country where you have options to choose from. I've been a few places, not a lot, but a few, enough to let me know that options aren't things most people have. Just make sure you take a step up. That's as important as anything. Believe that. A step up.

"Now, I'll tell everyone after work today. No need to do it through rumor. Since you're the only one who knows, I'll know it was you if word does get out."

Alberto and I walked slowly out of the dispatcher's shop and looked out over San Francisco. The city was about to go digital.

2.

Josephine and I had been making out in my room, and she wasn't stopping me from doing anything. Pulled her pants down, leaving her panties on for a moment so I could see how they fit on her body when she was naked. Pulled them a little more to reveal the first hint of pubic hair. All of my clothes were still on as she made no moves whatsoever to take those away. Did that myself. Undid her bra and finished the job on the rest, leaving her naked and me with more work to do by taking off the rest of my clothes.

Was so excited to have her naked lying next to me. The right music was on, and the record player wasn't skipping this time. San Francisco in the background. No vampires or goat-faced boys disturbing me. She moved my head down to give her pleasure, something I'd been waiting to do since we met. Got me so excited to be the one and only person to be doing that. Came just from the thought of what I was doing.

She rolled to her stomach.

"You know, when we used to make love, time stopped," Josephine said. "But I was the one who taught him things there. I was much more experienced than he was. That was the part of our relationship that balanced everything out."

She went on to tell me about everyone she had ever lain down with. The meth dealer whose breath smelled like menthol. The huge, muscle-goth guy who would hammer her so hard she would bleed. The gay guy she was sleeping with before me. The cheerleader in high school who used to come over sweaty from games and keep her skirt on.

Stopped her before she listed any more. Finally, the record finished, so I got up to keep my needle from wearing down.

"These are hard to find these days," I said. "More expensive, too."

We went on like that for the next few weeks, and as we did, I found out what caused her to cum and I made her each time, which made me happy and satisfied. Got the job done. Always concerned with that.

3.

Was lying in bed watching Josephine sleep and listening to the city burn through the fog when Kerri walked into my room holding a coloring book and sporting a look on her face that was searching for someone to blame.

"We need to move," Kerri said to Josephine, then turned me. "I'm looking today. This shit is too crazy. Why didn't you tell us?"

The sweet butterfly lashes knew that this would be the perfect moment to take her girl back. She didn't play the jealous role at all and let us have our fun, knowing that when you're doing that, your guard goes down. She was there for the long haul and waited to play her hand. Kerri knew Josephine well. Knew she wasn't seeing me at all.

"What are you talking about?" I said, not realizing I was being pulled out of my bubble.

"I saw Kurt on the street walking away with my jacket and Crayons," she said. "What the hell was he going to do with my Crayons? These people aren't in their right minds."

"Calm down, Kerri," Josephine said. "Come on and cuddle with us. There's room."

"The only place I'm going is downstairs to pack! She knew the whole time! How could you not tell us?"

"Tell us what?" Josephine asked, now waking up. "What's the matter?"

Kerri tossed her Winnie the Pooh spoon and hit me square in the forehead with it, cutting me a little, but nothing too serious. Josephine picked up the spoon and stared at the burnt black bottom.

"Wherever you want," said Josephine. "I trust you, Kerri. We'll get out of here. Together."

Making someone cum doesn't mean they're going to stay with you, it just means they'll stay happy with your tongue inside of them. Josephine turned away from me right there, and I knew she'd never return. Just like that, she was on her way out of my life.

It's like that, I think. Only a few stick with you down the entire way because on that path, there are so many missteps and falls that cause deep wounds and lasting scars, most people shy away when the pain starts. It's the ones who walk with you through it all that allow you to understand love.

You have to learn that by being left. It's the only way.

4.

Woke up alone, afraid to put my feet on the cold floor. Was totally out of socks. Nobody next to me to stay in bed with. No breakfast downstairs. No job to go to.

Alberto was on the other line making sure I was going to my interview. He had no idea about Josephine, and there was no reason to tell him. Had been up all night listening to Billie Holiday and Ella in hopes of feeling what they felt and having it heal me.

"You got everything you need?" he asked. "What are you wearing? Did you hook up your résumé like I told you to do?"

"You're making me nervous," I said. "Besides, there's no pressure here. We're trying to do something incredible. Just trying to do that is enough."

"It's not," he said.

I smiled and hung up.

Valerie walked in with a giant cup of coffee and sat down on the edge of the bed.

"You should have taken the whip job," she said. "Then you could just sit there and make your cute zines. Figure you'd be making about three hundred a night with that tight body of yours."

"I'm getting out of here," I told her, covering up as much as I could. "I don't want to be hooked like the two of you."

Valerie laughed and looked out the window into the same fog I was lost in.

"Kind of nice," she said. "Not being able to see anything. You should try it sometime."

"Don't need advice from someone who steals my socks," I told her. "Now just let me be. I've got a job interview today. Things are going to change."

"Things change regardless of if you try or not. Even in these jobs you're going after—I've heard things from some of my clients. Tons of investment going on in those places. Computers. People are through communicating through human touch. I'm kind of that last bit of the old guard. You've got to believe that somewhere, someone is always going to need people like me."

"Vampires?"

"Pleasure providers."

She finished her coffee and left. No doubt my reactions to her had little to do with who she was, but because of the emptiness that I was feeling from Josephine's absence. She and Kerri had left during the night—using a moving van and whatever help they could pay for to get the hell out of Dodge.

Have to say that was one of the things about Valerie that I really enjoyed and respected. She existed outside of the mainstream economy, ate directly off of the needs of the people. People paid big money to have their empty spaces filled in. Valerie would always have a job, but not the accumulated wealth to keep her alive past her prime.

At that moment I had two choices of what to join: the corporate world that would soon replace sitting in front of stacks of papers with sitting in front of a computer, or the underground life of sex dungeons. You may believe there's not that much of a choice, but think on it and tell me that your soul is any cleaner with the choice that you made to survive.

5.

Walked south of Market Street thinking about Valerie and what she was.

Day laborers were being picked up for jobs that nobody who was born in this country would do anymore. The pickup trucks made me think of those stories Valerie would tell me in the middle of one of her nods.

She was born outside of San Francisco, close to wine country. When her mother would take her on tours of the wineries, she'd always bring this one doll with her and drop it in the rows of grapes, forcing herself to pick it out, somehow always managing to scrape her thumb. When it bled, she sucked it dry.

Her mother was a reporter who could have gone anywhere in the country to write after she got out of school and finished with her internships. Turning down the big city papers on both coasts, she took up with a small paper in Wattsonville, a coastal town full of migrant workers, or those looking to be one.

Valerie spent her youth watching her mother poring over stories trying to give a face to those workers wearing masks vanishing behind rows of fruits and vegetables. You never see their faces on the packages in the frozen food aisles, but her mother did.

Her father couldn't take the choice, and after about a year of trying to make it as someone who fought for others, he decided he needed to take care of himself and moved to Chicago or some big city like that where he could disappear enough into anonymity by making good cash and eating in decent restaurants.

Valerie nerded out in high school and got a scholarship to go to Berkley but soon dropped out because she was learning more in the city across the bay than she was in the classrooms.

She met Darren D. one day backstage while he was sweeping up.

He was born in Hawaii, tall, skinny, and pale, so he naturally grew to resent the sun and all things tan. He came to San Francisco because he had sold some bad baking soda mixed with Raid and passed it off as coke to the son of a pretty powerful family.

Darren D. jumped the first flight he could find and ended up in San Francisco, but couldn't make it as a drug dealer in the club scenes out there, so he switched to heroin and found a good business shelling that out to the sex workers. It's always good to concentrate on the working class when you're distributing your product.

6.

Wasn't sweating because I was nervous, so it had to be the outfit I was wearing for the interview. Never wore things to show off my figure, but this time I geared a pencil skirt with a sleeveless blouse that kind of hugged my boobs enough to distract whatever man was going to be looking at me.

It's not all that tough to divert attention. The trick is not to show too much cleavage or they won't pay attention at all. I was a nice-sized C cup, so with the right gear on, guys couldn't help but look.

The man sitting across from me was looking at my résumé, then looking at me, then stealing looks at the women walking around in back of me. Place was an old warehouse like the ones we used to break into and Colin would tag up. All of South of Market Street was under development.

"See, we're part of the Internet revolution, but we're taking the back road!" he said, looking around as if there was somebody listening to a grand secret. "We've got millions coming in from VCs right now—you know what a VC is?"

"Viet Cong?"

He busted out laughing. "No, no, but that's great. See, we need people with that kind of sense of humor. You have to be able to laugh in the middle of the night when you're around these maniacs. Everyone calls me a maniac as well. 'There goes Belt David, he's totally insane.' That's what they say about me. That's what I want them to say about me!"

"You want people to think you're insane?" I half-asked, half-judged. "Not sure how people trust you with money if they think you're crazy. Guess that's why I'm sitting where I am and you're where you are."

That was the kind of backhanded-self-degradation-flipped-as-a-compliment that Alberto had armed me with prior to the interview.

"Yes—yes," he continued. "We're not looking for experience, see. We're looking for the right fit. For the right kind of people to come in here and give the products we help sell the right kind of face. We don't want office workers. We want creatives. We've got drugs to sell, you know."

"I know," I said. "As long as you don't test me for them, we're going to be just fine."

He leaned back and smiled. Inside, he was sure he'd taken another of us off the street and placed them right into his factory. He knew that most folks like me—those with tats or who wore Docs or who shopped at thrift stores because they had to and who wore vintage shirts because they hadn't bought anything new in a while—couldn't hold out on the fringe.

Looking around, you didn't see any ties. You saw jeans, Chucks, Mohawks, piercings, baggy jeans, skateboards—everything that was frowned upon in the corporate world was now being embraced. These guys were brilliant. They made everyone give up their bands and dreams of creating a small piece of themselves for the promise of an inflated paycheck and a chance to be on the forefront of the digital revolution.

"Come on, let's walk around so I can tell you more," he said. "I have a feeling you're going to fit in just fine."

Now, I have to say that, even though I knew I was going in undercover, the fact that this man was telling me I was going to fit in touched something inside of me. Nobody wants to be an outsider—nobody wants to be thought of as different or a freak—that just happens when the YOU that you are rubs folks differently from their beliefs and spurs fear in them. All of the freaks and outsiders, that's who were being recruited.

"So, we just won the digital business for Shaden Healthcare. You ever heard of them? No? Well, they just awarded thirty million dollars' worth of business this year to give them a presence on the Web. You're on the Web, right?"

"Never," I said, trying as hard as I could to seem as ambivalent as possible. "Hear everyone talking about it these days, but couldn't tell you much. Know a thing or two about computers though."

"That's fine," Belt said. "Anyone telling you they know too much about any of this is just bullshitting you anyhow. I want people here who want to learn. Who want in on this revolution!"

"Nothing like a good ol' revolt," I told him. "Where do I sign up?"

"Ha! Yes, you're just right for this," he said. "Now, for so long, the pharmaceutical companies have relied on paper in order to sell their products. Things like leave-behinds and pamphlets—I can see you don't know the terms.

"See, a leave-behind is something that pharmaceutical reps leave with doctors talking about what a specific medication does. They also leave tons of samples so the docs can hand them out to patients.

"Anyway, this digital revolution you see happening everywhere is spreading out into our world as well. That's the pharma world. They're asking us to create awareness campaigns on the Internet that cross over into other mediums. What this means is it's up to us to make people believe they have some sort of condition before they go in to ask their doctors about it.

"What the company we represent needs is to create these campaigns before the drug gets approval, so patients can go in and ask their doctor for a medication to help treat the disease they've been hearing about on the radio, newspaper, or TV. Just as the campaigns are really ramping up, the reps go in there and tell them about a new medication that treats this condition.

"If the awareness campaign works, people will start noticing little things about how they're feeling or acting. They go talk to the doctor and ask for some medication to help that out.

"Now, well, young people are going to start getting information from the Internet, so the drug companies are trying to get a presence on that medium. That's what we do! That's why you're here!"

"You create presence. I see," I told him. "What medications are you all representing?"

"Well, I can tell you only that we're bringing something new into the market," he said, licking his lips at the thought. "We are in the process of setting up the awareness campaign right now—and we're looking for the right minds to get behind it. I have a feeling that you have one of those minds."

My head was spinning. No doubt my mother had fallen victim to this type of campaign, and that forced her to have my pops go in to the doctor and ask for that depression medication.

Rather than react, I just nodded yes every now and then to what he was saying. Would come to find out that most people in offices have no idea what people are talking about, they just nod and say, "Yeah. Uh-huh. That's right. I hear ya. Totally." Just agree with what the person is saying to you and things are generally going to be okay. Alberto coached me up in office speak. He spent many years hanging around these places waiting for packages to deliver.

"What we want to do here," Belt said, sitting back on top of the counter in the makeshift kitchen, "what most of the new companies springing up want to do, is to create a culture. We want young people who understand how to communicate with other young people. It's no accident you're here. You know how to communicate without seeming like you want to. Are you interested in joining us?"

"Not sure," I said, trying to remain calm. "What kind of money are we talking about?"

He looked at me and tried to hide his smile. We were both hiding.

"I can start you off at 65K and some stock options. Full benefits, of course. We'll see what happens after that. Raises come quick to those who prove themselves indispensible. That'll happen by you being you, though—dress as you would and act as you would everywhere else. Nobody is going to judge you.

"We want you here, Sarah, that's what I want you to remember. It's you who is going to drive it. I could get some agency hack who uses the same tricks over and over again, but I want your mind—your ability to create. The music you listen to. You're going to connect to those kids out there who are growing up and about to enter the workforce. There is a boom coming, and they'll all be heading in."

That much a year meant I could help my pops and Alberto at the same time. I'd spend a few years in this place and keep producing the *Luddite* underground. The number of copies I could produce would be astounding.

More than that, I could get away from the vampires and out of that house.

Thing is, the guy behind the desk knew that. He knew that the outsiders needed a place to come in to and be safe—that he could get them, the ones who didn't have the plan like I did, to give up everything for that six-figure dream and help to medicate the country.

I accepted. We both thought we were playing each other.

7.

"I'll dis the facial nature of your ballywho."

—*Del the Funky Homosapian*

Took Alberto to Sparky's on Church Street. Fancy spot trying to look like a dive but had great people and a fantastic bookstore across the street that stayed open twenty-four hours and had a magnificent cat always decorating the window in slumber. Coffee. Smokes. Burgers. Everything that kept us going while the darkness did its thing on the outside.

Fog wasn't lifting. Stumbling people coming out to move their cars in their sleeping clothes looked like a zombie movie. Cars not given enough time to warm up moved slow and noisy through the streets looking for a safe place to park. The dealers were out early in Dolores Park.

Alberto had asked for a favor. Without his messenger gig, he was going to need some cash. No way he could go undercover—he would lose his cool too quickly—so he figured he could make some extra cash selling speed. Sworn off the stuff since Josephine—no need to feel like my chest was rocketing out of my rib cage.

Victor had hooked me up with his connect but made me promise to break him off some glass twice a week.

Paged the guy a few times, but he was slow in getting back. That's why we were waiting it out at Sparky's. Five hours later, at like six a.m., Alberto's pager went off.

Alberto rode me on the handlebars through the early San Francisco morning until we got to the start of the Mission District, but not really in the Mission District—a weird two-block stretch below Market Street on Valencia just after the freeway started. There were little patches like this that didn't have Victorian charm.

Alberto waited for me across the street and out of sight. Knocked lightly. Felt someone looking through the peephole at me before the door opened.

The man who answered went by the name of Dr. Richards and made sure you called him that. The first-floor, low-ceilinged apartment was illuminated only by an exposed red light bulb.

"Sit," he said. "Apologies for the delay in getting back to you. Business is booming for me these days. Can't keep up with the demand. You wanted coke, right?"

"Speed," I said. "Crystal if you have it."

"Easier to sell for profit," he replied, laughing. "Yeah, I see you. It's not for you. I can tell right off. You're not shaking or itching to get out of here. Patience is not really a trait of someone who's on the fiend. Am I correct?"

Didn't know how to answer. If he knew I was selling his product, he might see that as a threat and want to squash that quick. Had to play it smart, and since I couldn't tell what he was thinking, I played it even.

"My friends asked where I could get some—so, you know, I figured I'd pick it up and they'd let me party for free. Victor passed your number on. That's all."

"You're best to tell me the truth, because if you do that, we can talk business. If not, I'm going to sell it to you retail and then you'll be scratching to pick up leftovers instead of making it real for yourself. Don't worry about taking customers away from me. Coke is the big banger for me these days. With all these young kids raking mad cash, they want that magic white to take with them wherever they go. This shit you're asking for, that's for working-class folks, and I don't have time to deal with that. I'm more of a star man, myself. I like the connections that come with the upper class of slanging. Now, how much were you looking to get?"

"One bag," I said, thinking of how I could stock up with ramen and OJ with that small profit of what I'd sell it back to Valerie at. Was still a few weeks to go before I got my first paycheck.

He laughed and threw down a bag of crystal on the smudgy black table that he had pulled from the drawer below. It looked to be about as big as my index finger.

"That's some bullshit right there," he said. "I mean, you're here at this ungodly hour trying to make a little off the top and you're buying twenty bones' worth of meth? Come on, girl, think a little bit. You need to up your expectations. You buy in bigger quantity, your take-home profit is more, and you won't have to make as many trips to see me, which is better for me because I won't have to deal with this bullshit amount. Why don't you take an onion and see what you can do with it."

"I don't have money for that," I replied, not knowing what an onion was.

He leaned in and got serious for a minute.

"I'll give it to you on consignment. Three hundred. You break this into twenty-dollar grams and you'll clear one eighty on the bag. If you do it right, you might be able to unload it in a night. Who you selling it to?"

"Strippers," I told him.

He smiled, took away the small bag, and brought out the bigger one. He weighed it in front of me. One ounce exactly.

The onion.

Held it in my hand and moved it around a little. Looked like thousands of pieces of broken glass swooshing around. Kind of nice. We made arrangements for me to come back with the cash in a week, though Dr. Richard was pretty sure I'd be back sooner than that.

"Don't be going and making too much, girlie, or I might have to blast you and take over that for myself."

He busted himself up laughing and waved me off not to take him seriously. Wrapped the bag up in a Raider towel he gave me and placed it gently into Alberto's messenger bag, where Alberto had put so many of the business world's important documents no long ago.

Out the door and into the night again, a new product to deliver.

8.

Riding on Alberto's handlebars through the late night or early morning emptiness of San Francisco with an ounce of crystal meth in my backpack, heading towards his first delivery at Valerie's strip club in the Tenderloin. You'd think I'd be nervous about getting caught by the police, but I wasn't feeling that at all. We were both working again.

Was nice not to be in control, if only for a few minutes.

We turned left up Van Ness and headed north past the fancy music school where kids lucky enough to play, played on the steps. City Hall came and went quickly—the Roman-style building standing out against the rest of the reconstruction.

Right on O'Farrell, stopping at the theater. The guy at the door was wide awake, and he made us wait in the theater until he called upstairs. A girl danced out her routine onstage with a few people in the large theater looking because they had paid to look, but at this hour in the morning, they were searching for company more than anything else. You could tell that at one point, this had been the home of amazing burlesque shows and nights of memories, but that had deteriorated long ago.

Valerie came down and introduced herself to Alberto, then walked us upstairs. People were looking at me, at my bag actually, as Valerie took me into one of the back rooms.

"So, let's see what you brought," she said, not wasting any time. "Don't worry, it's safe. Besides, everyone is waiting on you. I kind of spread the word. Most of the girls here aren't working now anyway. They're here to make sure they can work tonight. If you have what I've been told you have in that bag of yours, well then, everyone's going to be happy."

Pulled out the bag wrapped in its towel and unwrapped it slowly, figuring that an unveiling of a product makes the product all the more valuable. Was a little mad at myself for not having broken it up into little bags already.

Opened the towel and revealed the ounce of broken glass. Valerie took a step back and smiled, revealing her fangs and some very alive eyes.

"That looks just amazing—but more than sixty dollars' worth."

"Yes—I got a little more than that. I can measure it out for you if you like."

"No, that's fine. I'll take the bag and sell it off here. How much?"

Was on the spot because I had no idea how much to charge for the bag. She could see that, so she reached into her purse and pulled out eight hundred in cash.

"That work?" she said.

Nodded. She took the entire bag and smiled.

"If it's good, and it looks amazing, I'll need you to come back on Friday with twice as much. I think people are going to enjoy this. Let me know. I think we're in business together, even if we're not going to live together. If you can get other things as well, I have other clients and other jobs, so there's always a need. Let's hope your connection is as thorough as you. This could turn into something nice. Anyhow, I'm on soon, so got to get ready. If you get a page from me, that means to bring two more on Friday. Stick around and watch if you like."

"We have to go," I said. "One thing, though: it's Alberto you'll be dealing with from here on out. Me, I'm going in for that gig. Couldn't turn down the money."

"You want to give all of this up?" Valerie said, motioning like she was revealing prizes on a game show. "That's fine. A messenger is a messenger. As long as it gets delivered, I couldn't care less."

She turned, but I could tell she was a little upset, just a little, that I wouldn't be in her life. No doubt she wanted to mentor me, but I never needed one of those.

Downstairs past the girls finishing up onstage, though Alberto didn't move as quickly. Having dropped off what we needed to deliver, we were free the rest of the morning, at least until I found out when my first day at the new gig was going to be. Outside, continuing our ride up the incline of Van Ness, the lightening sky lifted my mood. Newspapers were starting to get delivered to their boxes.

9.

Money in our pockets and the promise of much more. We reached the Marina where joggers were moving past and new mothers pushed their strollers, trying to look like they looked before they became mothers. A few high school kids who had no intention of going to class rolled joints. An old couple did their ritual exchange of newspaper sections in front of the water.

Alberto grabbed my hand, and we walked along the water until we reached the Buena Vista, which was filled with everyone you'd expect to find if a painter had gathered one of every kind of person in the city for an Edward Hopper moment.

The Buena Vista was one of those places in San Francisco that claimed the city for itself rather than let the city claim it. Made the first Irish coffee ever—used as something to help the dock-workers through years of systematically breaking their backs.

We walked in and joined the mosaic.

"Order what you like," he told me.

Ordered an eggs Benedict and he did the same, along with two Irish coffees. The sun was up outside and at our backs, and we were at a bar that had held up thousands like us over the years. Human.

The mirror showed Alberto smiling next to me, then glancing into the reflection to see what it looked like. Peeked for a moment myself. The coffees came and stretched out the white noise around us.

Bartender smiled.

"I've made a few drinks in my time," he said. "And if you don't mind me saying so, I think they have a bit of glue in there for those who are truly in love. I believe that's what I'm seeing in front of me, and what you're seeing in front of you."

He nodded at the mirror.

Warm all over from the whiskey and the breakfast with my best guy. Now we had the pleasure of strangers noticing us. Played with the illusion until breakfast was over and we walked along the steps that led into the bay. That area of the city was untouched by buildings or worries—unless of course you looked at the people folding into themselves and wondering what they needed to do to stand up once again. Guess the whiskey did different things if you drank it by yourself covered by a brown bag. A sublime sadness bounced off the bay.

He steadied his bike for me to sit on the handlebars. Leaned back slightly so I could feel the hardness of his chest against my back. Had ridden like this so many times with him that I knew how I fit in every part of his body. He started off. We passed by the old-timers still haunting the docks like ghosts in the fog, looking for their youth to come back but only seeing the lines and indents in their hands to remind them of what was taken from them. The fog only covered so much.

He increased his speed, and we continued on the strip that bends around, holding all of the piers that used to house ships but now only created an edge for the city. Past Pier 39—resurrected into an amusement park and shopping center.

Balloon-blowing clowns and unicycle riders stretched and got ready to entertain for the day, while a starting-to-hunch woman dragged her cart full of fruit past them towards the incline that led into North Beach. We probably could have followed that road, but we took the easy, longer way around to drink in the moisture of the fog and elongate the morning our moment was turning into.

The rest of the piers stood strong but silent as the old dockworkers milled about in their jackets, smoking over their cups of coffee and keeping low so as not to be swept away by progress. The lucky ones, if you want to call them lucky, got jobs as security guards protecting the grounds and waterfronts they used to own.

A middle-school couple kissed forever on the side of the wooden planks while tourists started lining up behind them for a chance to get tickets to head out to Alcatraz.

Never understood why a prison was such a fun place to visit.

We continued the ride. The fog was lifting in parts of the sky. The old fifties diner across from the bending road we were riding on had waitresses coming off their shift. Everyone was always getting off their shift in this city. We came around the final bend before Market Street dead-ended at the bay. The Greyhound bus terminal shuffled off junior high schoolers ditching school from the suburbs up north, and sending back people who couldn't fight the concrete.

Turning up Market, skateboarders, who never minded what kind of day it was, practiced their tricks while girls in hoodies sat hunched taking pictures, thinking they might be able to catch a moment and send it on in to *Thrasher* magazine.

Sounds of wheels on cement is universal.

Nine-to-fivers (or sixers, these days) headed into buildings, though they didn't push and shove each other for space. We rolled past the wall where all the bike messengers used to sit and wait for calls on their shoulder radios. I felt Alberto's chest shudder and heart beat heavy through his skin.

Making a right up Montgomery, where the hill inclined a bit, there was a different kind of business worker. Women wore tennis shoes with off-label skirts and their good shoes in the opposite hand of the lunches they were carrying. Buildings they were moving into were old and gothic, but nothing about them screamed retro. Had you removed them from the picture and put in the right kind of lighting, it would have made a perfect gangster movie.

Now to the top of Montgomery where the line starts to blur into Chinatown, you could see the men in the park playing games I could never understand while the women either waited for them or paid little attention to what they were doing.

Now up Columbus where the hill was steep. Alberto shifted to a down gear and started his push up. Could feel his heavy breathing and moved back as far as I could to be part of all of his movements. The bakery trucks were just finishing dropping off their goods, and the Lusty Lady's behind-the-glass strippers were finished and waited for buses or took cabs, depending on how well they had done that night. We stopped in front of the church in North Beach where I had taken Josephine.

The school bell rang.

With his face as dry as I could get it, I kissed him while giggles from the kindergartners came from behind the fence.

i.

My first day of work and I was excited. Had been staying with Alberto but not yet moved out of the vampire house. Slowly I was moving things into his place, which he had hoped to be permanent.

Layouts for *Luddite* were taking up space on his wall. He got up before me and made us a huge breakfast and woke me with a Duke Ellington Record. That big goofy smile was sun enough for me. Wish I loved him like he did me, but you can't force things.

Dressed in old Jordache jeans, a cut-up Guns N' Roses T-shirt, and a men's blazer. Didn't have to shop for any of it other than the G and R T-shirt, which I found for a buck at the Salvation Army because, at that time, it was out of style and not yet old enough to be vintage.

Alberto cooked up sunny-side-up eggs with some crispy hash browns and a buttermilk biscuit with gravy. Always thought that the way someone cooks for you is how much they love you.

The *SF Chronicle* was on the table talking more and more about the money coming into the city by venture capitalists. "New Gold Rush" was the headline.

Alberto and I went over our plans for how long it would take to get deep inside their world.

"To assimilate fully," he preached, "you have to appear as an outsider. They want to be the ones to bring you in. Never ask to be let in."

The Internet, whatever it was going to bring, promised to assimilate and dilute the last gasp of rebellion left in the country and consolidate all of the small truck stops and little diners along the back roads of this country into Burger Kings and Starbucks.

Wanted to call my pops before my first day, but it was too early for him, and lately he hadn't been able to come to the phone, anyway.

Alberto read the Metro section and pointed out a story about a homeless man who died sleeping out in front of the Ghirardelli Chocolate spot near the water.

Looked at my watch and enjoyed the fact that I had some-place to go. Enjoyed all aspects of the job, both the job itself and the fact that I was working undercover.

Summer disappeared into the cool fog of fall. Walked through the Mission at the same time little kids were on their way to school. Guess they start you out early to be up at a certain time each day to get to work. They were all carrying cute little bags with them, but I had nothing but my Walkman because I had been told not to bring anything with me into the office. Everything was going to be provided.

Made my way south of Market where the paint from the graffiti bombings not so long before was still fresh enough to be inhaled with the breeze. Outside the work spot didn't look any different than the other warehouses—but it's never the exterior that gives a true definition. The only office, if you could call it that, belonged to Belt. The rest was wide open space with long desks and those incredible chairs that, if my pops had ever worked in an office, I'd have spun around in for hours.

Guess the amount of open space would be the very thing that described it the best.

Looked over the group and saw that most everyone there had their own style—baggy-pants, long-hairs, pierced, tats, preppies, other, different kinds of folks—nobody looked the same.

Out of the corner of my eye, saw this familiar-looking kid spreading the cream cheese meticulously on one side of a poppy bagel.

"Colin!" I screamed out. "What the hell! What are you doing here?"

"Drawing," he said. "They needed someone who knew how to draw comic book characters. Said they wanted to reach into the 'hip-hop generation.' Showed them my book, and they hired me on the spot. Mad money. Bananas."

Was so happy to see him I didn't press or let on what I was up to. Figured, in some way, all of us felt that we were there only a little bit. That since they let us dress like we wanted and do whatever it is we did outside of the office, we could just take the money and run.

Belt David, the man who hired me, emerged from the crowd of free-food-eaters and was about to speak. Amazing how he just blended in before making himself noticed.

"You all know me because I'm the one who brought you in to PopCore," he started out. "You were, each one of you, chosen specifically because of your talents. You have filled a need, and now it's time to execute. Make no mistake about it, this is work and long hours, but we're going to be a family. You're going to contribute and be part of everything.

"We want you to create whatever you like—think the way you would on your own time. Just remember, anything you create here belongs to us. You are, of course, being well paid for those creations.

"Take time in your day to really get into your own ideas. Your ideas will help us grow, make our clients happy. It's a selling point for us. You actually *are* the company."

We were handed seating charts and found our desks, and each had a new computer front and center. As we sat down, you could tell everyone was wondering what to do next.

"How do you turn this thing on?" I asked Colin, who either had magically gotten the seat next to me or decided to take it on his own.

"Not a clue," he answered. "Never had one before."

"Neither have I," I said.

Similar phrases echoed around the room. Turns out that nobody had ever owned a computer, much less sat in an office behind one.

2.

After they ordered us lunch from House of Nanking, we were all instructed by a man with a medium-sized afro, with his keyboard in his lap, to turn to the south wall of the office, which, we soon found out, was used to project presentations. The words "Disease Awareness" was a global element on every screen.

Belt stepped forward.

"Three letters," he said. "Three letters are going to be what you're concentrating on for the next few months. ADD. Attention deficit disorder."

In front of us on the round tables were folders containing the creative brief. I looked around to see all of these graffiti writers and hipsters holding these official documents. Nobody knew what to do with them. Belt didn't care. He knew everyone was smart enough to catch on quick. He'd make executives out of us all in no time—it was, after all, the easiest thing to become once you knew the right terminology.

"The CTA—that's 'call to action,'" he said, realizing that nobody understood any of the secret words that people used to show they understood a specific industry. I remember what Valerie said about not really needing to know anything, you just need to know what the letters stand for. Don't try to fake it, either—because when people say an acronym, they check your pupils to see if you know what they're talking about.

He went on.

"We need to get people talking about ADD. We're going to target teens a year away from entering college and those in their first few years of school. That is the arc we are looking at. The sweet spot. You all—each of you—are going to help us hit it.

"I want to introduce you to Kimberly Most. She is, for all intents and purposes, the client. She works for Shaden Healthcare."

Kimberly walked to the front of the room and everyone stopped. The sounds of her shoes went in perfect rhythm with each of her movements. The guys were drooling. Inside, have to admit, I was drooling a little bit as well.

"So glad to have all you people involved with this campaign," she said, resting up against the back wall. "We've put a lot of resources into this already, and we know you're going to provide a magnificent return on our investment."

A picture of what looked like a café, but with computers on every table, was on the next slide.

"You'll start to see these popping up all over the city," Kimberly continued, catching me looking at her and holding that look before continuing. "San Francisco is a good test spot for that.

"For the past year, we've be doing studies with our KOLs. Now these key opinion leaders are doctors who are on our payroll and perform 'observation studies' that allow them to write the papers that will serve as the foundation of fact.

"We constructed replicas of these Internet cafés and used them to study how seventeen- to twenty-year-olds react to being in front of computers and online for extended periods of time. Some of the subjects studied are runaways or have been remanded to juvenile facilities—their guardians signed waivers granting them early release if they participate in the studies."

Next slide.

"We've installed cameras to monitor the usage of the machine and track who is logging in and how long they stay on. We track how long they pay attention before feeling the need to jump to another webpage. Over a few months, they've been studied to see if there has been an increase in lack of discipline, hyperactivity, impulsivity, et cetera. It's all been documented and published in peer-approved journals.

"Being in front of computers and connected to the Internet over a certain period of time tended to impair the subjects' ability to concentrate on one subject for very long. Our KOLs decided to call this disorder ADD—attention deficit disorder.

"Shaden Healthcare has developed a medication to help treat this disease. The market name for it will be Atendol. The awareness campaign you create is going to help people understand the disease they have, and drive them to go to their doctor and ask for a prescription.

"Any questions?"

Raised my hand. Belt smiled, and Kimberly nodded at me.

"You're creating the disease, though, right?" I asked. "If you didn't sit those people in front of computers, they'd be just fine. You're creating the disease as well as the cure."

Belt stepped in front of that bullet.

"It's the digital revolution that's creating the disease," he said. "What we're doing is helping people acclimate to it.

"Let's be clear: This is the industry we're in. Very few people know as much as Kimberly just told you. If word got out and we found out that that any of you were responsible, imprisonment would be a definite possibility. You should have no illusions about what you were getting into. You all signed nondisclosure agreements."

We all knew that we were entering something that was pulling us away from who we really were. Think every job that you have to take is like that. Myself, I was there undercover—but I still didn't want to be there. None of us did. You tell yourself it's only for a little bit—until you have enough saved up or paid bills or taken care of the people you need to take care of—whatever your reason is for taking the money they offer you for coming in. They entice you like you're doing them a favor by joining them— that your talents are somehow needed to keep them going. That you, *you* are the missing piece to their success. They lie to you, and you lie to them. That's the exchange.

We broke into three teams. Strategy. Creative. Development.

Wish I had gone with Colin into the creative department, but they wanted me on the strategy team. Guess it was good. Being comfortable with a friend at work could have distracted me from what I was there for. Money and information. Don't forget that.

3.

SEO (search engine optimization). That's the big ticket. Always has been.

Back in the day, before all of you were buying your books on how to optimize your website, companies like PopCore were studying how people search online by watching actual people do it.

When you type something like "ADD" (or whatever may be dominating the market at the time you're reading this) into your search engine, see what comes up. What's at the top of the page? It's not information about the disease—it's an advertisement for the drug company that wants you take to its medication. It may be a site dedicated to talking about ADD and how it can affect your life, but I'll guarantee that site was created by a drug company.

Awareness. Creating awareness—creating panic—creating the need for a cure.

Was excited not only about all of the inside information I was scooping up for *Luddite*, but about being back in an actual learning environment for the first time since high school. Some went to college to be well-rounded. Me, I was getting paid to drug the country. Better than that, was getting paid to subvert it.

"This is your brand book," Kimberly said to our team. "Think of it as a bible. It's the law. If it says so in here, it's not changing. Anything not in here, that's your territory. We're going out to a testing center tomorrow so you can see subjects and ask questions. Until then, enjoy the day."

Got home—Alberto's home—took off my boots and skirt, leaving on only my T-shirt.

Started reading the ISI (important safety information) for Atendol. This was, by law, required to be written on every piece of material talking about the drug. It told about all the rashes, liver conditions, dizziness, and other catastrophes that could happen if you took the drug. True, it's on everything, but nobody likes to read too much.

The one for Atendol explained how the product was tested on monkeys who had previously self-administered cocaine. Now that was something I'd be really be into seeing.

No doubt there are thousands of teenagers around the country who would love to see monkeys sitting around a table doing lines. That's all people wanted to see anyway: vampires, monkeys, and expensive drugs. Thing is, if you promise those things on the outside of the circus tent, you'll get the audience in to educate them.

Couldn't help but think about my dad and the anti-depression medicine that that my mom had made him take.

Picked up the phone to call him, but got the machine.

Door swung open, revealing Alberto again. He was sweating like crazy. Threw a big wad of cash on the table, but he wasn't happy.

"They're taking us to the labs," I told him. "Think of what we're going to see. You were right!"

He slouched at the table we had set up.

"Thought you'd be more excited," I said, taking out some bread and cheese—the only way I knew how to cheer a man up and stay happy myself at the same time. "You were totally right. I'm getting deeper in."

"I have nothing to do during the day but make money selling this shit," he said. "Without riding, I've got no balance. Money doesn't give that to me."

"I'm doing the same thing," I told him.

Grabbed him tight and felt him shaking. That sturdy body I leaned up against had lost a little bit of weight. The scars on his legs weren't healing. "You better not be using that shit," I said.

To be a dope man, you must qualify,
Don't get high off your own supply.

—*NWA, 1989*

He got up and went to the bathroom, taking my dry cleaning for the next day of work off the hanging door and placing it nicely inside the closet.

CHAPTER 12

i.

Cream silk blouse, winter white cardigan, nude stockings with a pinup line down the back, a T-shirt I bought from the young men's department at Ross, and a good pair of Mary Janes. The day of my first corporate event, so I wanted to be at the office early.

Belt was already there, smoking a cigarette outside and looking into the window of a pickup truck parked on the side of the road.

"They don't make them like this anymore," he said, seeing me approach in the rearview.

"They don't make anything anymore," I replied. "Seems like that's going to be a problem."

He looked up and half smiled, but I think it was to himself as a congratulations for hiring the right person. That's the thing about working there—I could be myself undercover.

"How's that?" he said. "Who's not making anything? We're creating systems that should allow for communications to reach so far beyond what we've done before. You think these pieces of metal are more powerful than what we're doing?"

"It's air," I told him. "We'll be making Nikes for teenagers in China before too long. Gothic punks in Beijing are gonna be hating on the cool kids for wearing Jordans. 'Think of those Americans working twelve-hours days for twenty-five cents an hour!' they'll say in pity as they carry protest signs with posters of sweatshops in Austin, Texas, taped to them."

2.

The secretary behind the desk was of the old regime of offices—guess the change had not reached out of the reaches of the city.

"Which study are you here for?" she asked, as if we were driving up through a drive-through picking out value meals.

Grabbed one of the brochures on the desk.

Trajectory Facilities—A Moderate Place

Our comfortable examination rooms allow you to monitor your subjects in an environment you create and control. We provide full food services in the viewing rooms, and our deluxe rooms come equipped with a full bar, resting couches, and docking stations for your computer equipment.

Our state-of-the-art video recording facilities are designed for times when viewing your subjects in real time isn't enough. Your marketing team needs time to reflect, process, and interpret every action. Created by the same team that developed instant replay for NBC Sports, our facilities allow you to focus on individual body parts and see how your subjects react to what they see.

*While many companies bring their own behav-
ioral psychiatrists with them, Trajectory Facilities
also makes available our own professional staff
to sit in with you and help analyze what your subjects are feeling and thinking.*

Before I could finish, we were being led down the hall to our
viewing room.

Inside, the smells of fresh coffee and an omelet bar welcomed
us. Kimberly was sitting right up on the glass bar. Next to her was
Tim Folden, one of the account people from their office. In the
days to come I'd learn he was a good guy on his own, but he was
rarely alone. He talked about his shoe collection all the time and
was always wearing the newest Jordans. Good guy and smart,
but he always folded into himself when his boss, the lead account
person Audrey Flexor, was next to him. She sat uncomfortably
close to every man she could in hopes of catching a touch.

Audrey had been in the pharma game for a long time and
had the good bank account (but empty home) to show for it. She
never stopped talking other than to whisper to Tim, who looked
like he was holding in his sickness at the warm breath seeping
into his ear. She had tons of power because, though she worked
for the agency, she was embedded with the client, which meant
she had an office there so she could deal with the day-to-day pan-
dering and ass-kissing required to keep a client happy. Made herself indispensible, and more than that, nobody else wanted to be
her. She talked with Kimberly and smiled wide like a horse does,
showing its teeth to its master.

The door opened, and a short woman with pencils behind
each of her ears and a clipboard pressed against her chest entered
the room, followed by her assistant, who tried to grab a bagel but

was immediately ordered out of the room, only to appear on the other side of the one-way glass.

The room looked like a pimped-out version of the inside of those control booths they used to cut to in the middle of Monday Night Football games I'd tape and watch with Pops when he came home. Monitors and cameras everywhere.

"Good morning, everyone," she said. "I'm Tracy. I'll be moderating your subjects today. They're all here and being served breakfast, though not quite as nice as what you're all eating."

Half of us laughed.

"Anyways, they won't be able to see you or hear you, but I ask you to keep your voices down as there is something to be said for the energy that negativity or mocking voices can cause. I'll ask a series of questions, then come back here after they answer and find out if there is anything I've missed. So, if you're ready to begin, I ask that you take your chairs and we'll get going. You'll find a program at each of your stations giving you backgrounds of each of the patients so you can put them in context and keep your imaginations from running wild."

She vanished behind the same door she had sent her assistant out of and appeared in the next room. Belt sat close up against the glass and was checking his program to see who would be first in. Tim tried to move closer to me, but Audrey shadowed his move.

"I hope we get to see the monkeys today," I said to Tim, taking a bite of my pancakes. "That's the show I'm here for."

"You don't want to see that," he said. "Trust me there."

"What's that?" Audrey said, leaning over and exposing the freckled boobs that hung out of her inappropriate dress. "You want to let me know what you're talking about?"

"She asked where the bathroom was, Audrey," Tim said, saving both of us from having to hear any more from her. Inside he was a good guy, but he'd bought into office life and was too far gone to save for real.

The first person came in. He was a teenager with a lip ring, perfectly fitted oversized gray hoodie, and an Oakland A's hat turned to about twenty degrees to the left of center. He leaned back in the chair after shaking hands with the moderator.

"How's your day going?" she asked. "Have you been getting everything you need?"

"I'm hella nice right now," he said, licking his lips and smiling halfway. "Been getting paid to play video games for, like, three months nonstop, and now you all are giving me a bonus to sit here and talk. Gotta love that. Mom was a little shy about it at first, know what I'm sayin'—but she's cool with the cash I'm bringing in. *Hella* nice."

"That's good," Tracy said calmly, crossing her legs as she hit the last syllable of the D in good. "Was wondering if you'd like to do a little more with some computers. We've got a few things we'd like you to look at."

She turned on the computer in front of him. From each of the monitors around the window, we saw how different body parts reacted. Pupils. Finger-twitches. Foot-taps. Hell, there was even a crotch cam to see how sexually stimulated they got.

She started showing him a bunch of primitive websites with different colors and various forms of navigation, each time asking him how they made him feel. He had been playing Internet-based games in test labs for the last three months, so he was used to navigating a computer.

After about fifteen minutes, she stopped writing things down and put her clipboard down. From under the desk she pulled out a newspaper.

"What section do you like?" she said. "I need to go make a phone call real quick."

"I'll take the sports page," he said. "See what's up with the Warriors."

She took out the sports page and laid it in front of him.

"Do me a favor," she said. "Read one article, any article you like, and when I come back, tell me what you think about how it was written."

Tracy smiled and walked out the door. A few seconds later, she came into the viewing room and sat next to Belt after putting on her headset.

"Can I get a close shot of the eyes, please?"

The camera zoomed in on his eyes, and we watched him on the monitor like it was a TV show as he started to read the paper. Going through the article, his hands started twitching a bit. He jumped to another. Then to another—he'd usually get two sentences in, then stop.

He jumped right back on the computer and started opening and closing websites, never staying on one for too long. There were clocks timing how long he stayed on each page and what links he clicked to go to the next.

"Doctor," Tracy said. "Do you think this young gentleman would be easy to diagnose as someone who would have attention deficient disorder?"

"Indeed," the doctor nodded, seeming to come out of the unnoticed shadows of the room. "He exhibits all of the symptoms required by the FDA for such a diagnosis. Let's move him to stage one of our clinical trials. I'll let you all work out the monetary compensation. Let's move on to the next."

Tracy went back into the room, opening the door slowly enough to allow the kid to grab the paper and pretend like he'd been reading it the whole time.

"Sorry about that," she said. "I've gotten called away and need to cut this a little short. You can stop by the receptionist and pick up your compensation."

"I get paid the same as if I did the whole thing, right?"

She smiled. "You do. In fact, we might have some other events for you to attend, if you're interested. Martha will explain everything out front. Thank you so much for your time."

She shook his hand and went to her clipboard, allowing him to happily leave and go collect his check. Of course, inside the check would be a release form to participate in the next step of the clinical trials.

Throughout the day, the same interview took place with kids right around our age. All of them had been in some sort of game-playing or Internet café setting for the past three months, and now the effects were being tested. Tracy spoke in the same tone to each of them.

Lunch got served, but there was no break from the patients walking in. The one-way mirror turned into a TV show, and pretty soon people were making jokes and commenting on the poor saps on the other side of the glass. Could have been any of us being watched as well.

CHAPTER 13

i.

Three a.m. Kinko's. Putting the *Behind the Mirror* zine together. Alberto was serving clients while Colin and I folded the pages and stapled the binding. Because of the new cash flow, I was able to use better paper for the cover and produce greater quantity. Could see that Colin was a little more fidgety than normal, but I'd been living with Alberto for a bit, so fidgety kind of made sense to me. My eyelids were so heavy.

Alberto offered me a line, but after that day with Josephine in North Beach, I'd sworn off powders forever. Couldn't tell Alberto to stop, seeing as how I was helping to sell pretty much the same thing but with a fancier name and a bigger budget for marketing. Still, I knew what being around such things would eventually do.

"You know," I said, "with the money I'm bringing in, you don't need to be selling speed anymore. Can't have both of us being drug dealers."

He grabbed me and kissed me under the awful florescent lights at Kinko's. Guys in the blue shirts and khaki pants seemed uninterested. Kissed him back, but it wasn't for real. He tried not to know that, but was too smart not to.

The door opened harshly, bringing in the November chill. Valerie.

She'd been crying. Alberto turned away from me.

"Need to work a double tonight and I haven't slept in two days," she said. "Can I get fifty worth?"

"Tell you what," Alberto said. "I've got, at cost, about five hundred in that messenger bag over there. Pay me that and it's yours. Should last you weeks if you do it right."

She reached into her army jacket and pulled out a crumpled wad of cash, peeled away five hundred, and tossed it on the lighting board.

"Mind if I take the bag as well?" she said. "Need something new to carry my stuff around in. Darren's blood spilled over my last one."

Hadn't noticed to that point, but she had been carrying a stack of notebooks under her arm when she walked in the door.

"He's gone," she said, jumping up on the table. "Final act of the tragedy for him."

She looked out the window like she was watching to see if she could catch his spirit crossing over to the other side.

"I was never one for partners, you know, but that man was part of me. Nobody else really understood him, and they thought that he was a user—just wanted my cash and the lifestyle I could provide—but thing is, he fit me. There won't be another like him. Maybe I'll get clean."

"What happened?" I asked.

"You'd think it was an OD," she said, sighing. "But I don't think there was anything he could put in his body that he couldn't handle. That's for sure.

"He was on the bus and tried to pick up this little kid he thought was cute. Was always into those little boys with saggy pants. Anyhow, he made a few looks and tried to start up a conversation. Kid played him perfectly. Walked with him into an alley, and just before Darren was about to get pleasure, kid stuck a knife right into his side and left him there.

"By the time they brought him into the hospital, he'd already bled to death. What you see on me is what rubbed off when I hugged him for the last time."

She picked up the messenger bag and patted its side.

"You know," I said gently, trying not to feel Alberto's wince. "If you ever want to put that down, I'd be glad to put it in an issue of *Luddite*. Might be a proper memorial for him. You could add something to what we're trying to do."

"That's sweet," she said, clearing the last bit of eyeliner from her left eye. "But I don't write what's happening. I am what's happening. Besides, you already have what you need. You've been watching it all. That's the kind of person you are. That's your drug. Intake. This man with you, he's using you for your intake. At least Darren was up front about what he wanted."

"I don't want anything from this girl!" Alberto said. "You're the one that stole everything from her. You're just a fucking junkie. Nothing more."

Valerie turned to leave, then put herself together. "Life is not over yet," she whispered. "No need to go and make absolute comments. By the looks of you, you're closer to me than you think."

Holding Alberto's messenger bag under her arm, she made her way out the door and disappeared in the night.

We continued slicing and stapling.

2.

Started getting to the office earlier each day. You spend more time with these people than anyone else, so it just kind of becomes your family.

The ADD drug was still a few months away from getting approval from the FDA, but we'd been at the awareness campaign for going on four months now. The creatives were stuck in concepting rooms, where they'd pitch each other ideas and fight it out over the best way to deliver the messages. Of course, it was the strategy team who decided the delivery, but we were told to let the creatives fight it out among each other, then take their product and fit it to what we needed. They always got pissed because they were artists, but as soon as you start selling your talents to the highest bidder, you let go of your right to stand up for yourself.

After all, advertising is all about selling product. Creativity should be driven by strategy.

Felt bad because Colin was on that side, but he knew this was just a money grab and had no illusions that the work he was doing had anything to do with art.

Most of these people had been writing music or bombing the streets with graffiti, so they brought that passion with them into the office and battled it out. Always good for the company to have its employees so invested in each idea. None of them ever realized that their battles were not worth fighting. They were just helping to narrow down a concept.

Tim was the go-between with all of the departments. No matter the problem or missed deadline, his response was always "I hear ya" or "Couldn't agree with you more." At the end he'd then just make you do what Audrey told him to do and then come hunched over to the creative folks and pass on what he'd been told, trying to give himself an air of authority. Frustration was usually the first reaction to such go-arounds, but everyone eventually became accustomed to getting overruled, and they just did their jobs with the expectation of getting shot down.

Thing is, it worked out well. The amount of people you need to create just the right amount of corporate madness makes for a nice billing sheet to present to the client.

Each day, Colin would come in, put his jacket on the back of his chair, turn on his computer, and let out the same sigh.

Weeks and weeks of studying people behind one-way glass, followed by data-dump sessions. Belt taught us, stressed to us, that once we understood how people searched for information, we'd be able to target them and sell our message when they were on the hunt for information. Once we knew the pathways, we could create parallels to lead Internet users to information about ADD.

All of this would be recorded and put into the next issues of *Luddite* and distributed across the country one by one, person by person. It didn't matter how long it took. These were going to be physical documentation of the truth. With all of the new Internet companies popping up everywhere, nobody would be looking at something stapled together in the untold hours of the morning to be bringing the truth to the world.

3.

Alberto had promised to kick the speed. It was early morning, and I made sure to wake up before him. Earlier that week, I had bought him a new messenger bag and put the zines inside them. Laid it on the table for him so that when he woke up to the smells of breakfast, he would have a present for himself. It's good to have surprises in your life.

His eyes opened, and he stumbled to the table, then paused when he saw the bag.

"This is what you've wanted," I said. "Now I need you to get the word out to more people. If we're going to be spending money producing, you're going to have to pull your weight with the distribution. You've got product—go slang. Talk with people. Make friends with every local shop and owner. Tell them what this is about. Network. Deliver. It's your time."

His nose was red and a little raw, but his eyes melted goodness all over his face. Moved his right hand, shaking a bit, over the bag as if he was examining the contents from above.

"Take a look at this," I said, handing him the bound notebook with the data recovered from our studies at the lab. "We just need to make it digestible for a wider audience. Let's get these numbers out there."

"Little light reading for me?" he joked. "What gives?"

"You were right, Alberto," I told him, balancing on the table to get my boots on. "Drugging everyone in every way possible. Even feel it a little bit. Just sitting in front of that computer, when I get up, I just want something else to look at. Can't wait to get in front of it again, not going to lie to you about that. You seen my MUNI pass?"

"You're too strong to get sucked into that," he said, putting the new messenger bag over his shoulder. "We'll have what we need soon enough, then you can break out of there. Don't get too into it."

"You just stay out there with the bikes and zines, Alberto," I told him. "We need someone away from this damn digital revolution putting out the word. They'll never be looking for us there."

"You saved me," he said.

"I know."

Gave him a kiss because it was the right thing to do in the moment and went to work. It was client day at the office.

4.

Everyone at the office was ready to kiss some ass. Two dudes from Shaden came in dragging these little rolling suitcases behind them. Kimberly led the team in wearing a two-piece skirt suit with a white shirt underneath so perfectly ironed it looked like she had been prepped by a group of fashion photographers. Think my body was as good as hers, but she just knew how to put her clothes together to fit it so well.

One of them had gone out and bought a new pair of Levi's because he knew he was coming to the city to see us. Our PR team had done an amazing job of getting a report together about our unusual approach to the corporate world, and how that might actually change the way business is done and how people interact at the office.

The other guy had a crew cut and his shirt tucked in past his almost skinny belt but not-so-flat stomach. Probably was a line-backer in high school who loved to "light people up" and never got over it. Handed me a card—name was Zachary Lefforts—and made it a point that he wanted to be called Zachary.

"We got word that the FDA is going to announce approval in the next two months," Kimberly said proudly. "Let's start with the girls and the gays. Strategy reports it has the greatest cost-benefit analysis."

The way she said "benefit" with her tongue hitting the roof of her mouth and clicking on the T—it made me excited.

"Once we get them, everyone else follows, right?"

Everyone agreed with Kimberly. See—she had been a warrior back in the days of the big drug hustle, sitting in waiting rooms of doctors' offices with free samples and round-trip tickets to various islands where medical conferences were being held about new drugs that needed a few KOLs (you know the terminology now).

You wouldn't think about this when you're sitting in the waiting room of your local doc, but what they have in their magical little cabinets or what's waiting for you on the other end of those prescriptions is a result of how well people like Kimberly hustle.

She knew how to command a room, and she knew what the docs wanted and, honestly, knew just the right time to cross her legs. Men get shook by that kind of thing. That's the triple threat in a pharmacy world filled with people who never really did what they wanted to do with their lives. Face it: who says as a child that they want to go out there and help sell drugs to people who don't need them?

Well, guess when you put it like that, there are tons of people in the world who sell and buy utterly useless objects, but thank goodness they do. If not, the thrift stores would be empty.

Kimberly took off her jacket and started drawing up on the big dry-erase board. Zachary and Bill rolled up their sleeves as well, getting ready to do some serious work. Kimberly wrote two words on the board:

Girls and Gays.

We broke into two groups to tackle each. They, of course, put me in the girls group. Nice. We all sat around talking about what eighteen-year-old girls were most interested in and how we could get them to believe that they were affected with ADD. Whatever we said went up on the board. The calls came out quick and furious from our group, which was full of guys who wanted nothing else but to talk about eighteen-year-old girls.

Panties. Sex. Boys. Makeup. Cars. School. Leaving home. Clubs. Drugs. Magazines.

Slowly, the conversation turned into jokes about eighteen-year-old girls and why each of these guys was waiting for whatever girl they knew to turn eighteen or what high school girl they had seen on the MUNI. Started going off on tangents about going to jail and them selling this drug in jail. Little jokes.

Then on to TV episodes. "Did you see that episode of WKRP in Cincinnati when…?" Or, "Did you see that movie where the tutor totally sleeps with that young guy?" They talked about scenes for lengthy periods of time.

Who in their right mind wants to hear someone else recite lines from movies and television shows? Is this what had been going on in offices all this time? Did people really spend the better part of their lives living like that?

It was spiraling out of control and didn't stop. Pizza was served. The room got sweaty. Nobody was listening to anyone. Everyone was just tossing ideas out there and talking to hear their own voices—trying to figure out a way to get girls about to be women to realize that they had ADD.

Belt sat there listening, waiting to chime in last because every vet in the game understands that you need to wait until all the crap is spit out to come in at the end, take the pieces that were tossed out there, and make it into gold.

"Look," he said. "For the traditional route, we can get some stories planted on the evening news about the growing concerns parents have about their children's ability to concentrate after spending so much time in front of the computer.

"For the teens, it's the Internet itself that's going to actually inflict the disease. For them, the Internet is that underground. They think they are only a modem away from some kind of uprising—a secret world where information can be exchanged without anyone regulating. However, it's going to be just like in the sixties, when 'Peace and Love' was thought to be the revolt, but it was really the co-opting of a movement. They'll be running to the Internet thinking they're breaking away, but really, they won't be able to concentrate on a thing. They'll develop into the adult office population, and it will be passed on for generations to come."

"How are we going to make them believe they're suffering?" Zachary asked. "The key to our success is for them to go in to their doctors and ask for it. 'Doc, I can't concentrate. I might have ADD! What do you have for that?'"

"That's the beauty," Belt said. "The name itself. It's fun to say, easy to remember, and most of all, it's an excuse to fuck up."

"What if we infiltrated?" I said, unable to help myself from jumping on Belt's thought. "I mean, what if we got in there where these kids were hanging out and just infiltrated their scenes? We could spread the word that way. Some of us would just go in there and start dropping the word ADD. Others, well, we could sell drugs, some kind of speed that could create the condition from the inside. I'm sure Shaden has something cooking in their labs that can cause the symptoms of ADD to surface. Then it would be a world of children on speed and computers that would cause the disorder. We could run media reports on how these things that are now so entrenched in our world are affecting each and every child out there. Hell, parents would be running to the doctors and begging them for something to help their children. It'll be perfect. We'd own the market forever."

"Well, not forever, I'm afraid," Kimberly said, smiling and impressed. "See, you can only hold the patent on something for so long. After a while, anyone can make the drug, and then it goes by its generic name—and at a much lower cost. Owning the patent is everything."

"What happens when it goes generic, then?" I asked. "I mean, you all have to lose tons of cash once that goes down."

"Well, we start working on something similar, but a little different, a few years before that happens. We change around a molecule, and then we can call it something different. You'll be working on that soon enough, but for now, I really like how you think. Do you really think that kind of infiltration you were talking about is possible?"

Laughed inside because I'd made up the most absurd thing I could think of to get inside those labs. It might have been that I wanted to get closer to Kimberly as well. You just started saying things like that in meetings.

Just had to see those goddamn monkeys! In order for that to happen, I needed full access. Kimberly had full access.

CHAPTER 14

i.

Kimberly took me to this spot up on Russian Hill to discuss how we were going to implement the plan. It was April, and one of those rare times of the year when the evenings in the city allowed you to wear whatever you wanted and the wind and fog wouldn't really get to you. The streets up there still had indie coffee houses and non-chain stores leaning against each other. She ordered the right kind of wine to go with the meal (which she also chose). Took a long sip, just kind of leaned back and watched her close her eyes.

"You know, I can tell what you think about me," she said. "Thing is, I've already thought all of those things and gotten past them."

She reached for a piece of bread, felt that it was cold, and called the waiter over to ask for another, all while keeping her eyes on me.

"Where are you from?" she asked. "I can still see wherever it is on you."

"Kansas City," I told her, proudly.

She smiled and retracted her aggressiveness just a bit.

"I used to be from somewhere as well," she said. "Now I'm just a part of this city. I don't mind, though. San Francisco is an incredible place to just kind of escape to and reinvent yourself. That's why you came out here?"

Knew she was trying to dig inside of me and see who I was and what I was up to. Nobody ever just up and talks to you like that—engages in a conversation for the sake of getting to know you. Everything is a pause and a thought.

"Came out here to get paid," I told her, figuring that it was pretty much the truth, and people like her can tell if you're lying anyhow. "That and to be part of what's happening out here. It's kind of amazing. All of these people who were tossed out of their hometowns for being too crazy or whatever you want to call crazy—different, I guess. They all come here and it's their home. It's a cradle."

The waiter put down some brochette and shaved fresh parm over it. Got to say that after months of eating burritos and other food that could be eaten by hand, it was a unique pleasure to see something presented on a plate.

She didn't wait for me to grab my piece. Each bite was followed by a balanced sip of wine.

"Most of them think I'm a bitch," she said, waiting for enough of the food to be swallowed. "Me, I don't care much what other people think. Grew up watching my mom clean up houses of people just like the people I now manage. Worked two jobs in school while everyone else was out drinking and partying like crazy. There was no problem for me going after the big money. I knew these people didn't care much about themselves because their parents would always be there with a bailout plan. Fuck 'em."

"I never got bailed out by anyone," I said.

"I know that," she replied, glancing the tip of her shoe against my calf and then apologizing while watching my reaction. "That's why your ideas are better than the rest's. They have to be. Watch yourself, though. People with the best ideas are the ones to get their throats cut."

We held looks and drank wine right there in the middle of the day. Whose side was I on? This woman was making as much sense as Alberto. Missed my pops right there. Sometimes in the middle of looking for people to love and admire, it's the people you came from that you need to speak with, but they're never around.

Across the street, a group of kids were at the bus stop tagging up the glass with black shoe polish that dripped down as they wrote. In the back of one of their pockets, I saw a copy of *Luddite*.

"Those are the people we need," Kimberly said. "That's what you were thinking, right?"

"You read my mind," I told her. "We'll work good together."

We finished the glass, then a bottle, and then another. Shifted from work to life to family to semi-secrets that you can't help but disclose when you feel the need to be close to someone.

2.

Being tight with Kimberly gave me more freedom. Had the research groups at my disposal, and we started to hone in on just how to go after a target population.

Belt wanted to keep Kimberly happy, so he allocated decent parts of the budget to help put my strategies into play. He thought it would be a good idea for me to go with Kimberly to the Shaden Healthcare testing labs so I could see how strategy gets implemented on the ground level of research.

Excited, because I was even closer to seeing the monkeys, what I had been after since I'd read the "Important Safety Information." Shaden was located in a high-gloss glass building in downtown San Francisco.

"My office is up on the seventh floor," she said, "but we're going to go and see the labs today and find out what they might have to help put your plans into action. This man walking up to us right now can pretty much help create what we need...Dr. Fidrych, how are you today?"

Dr. Fidrych had a thick nameplate and an even thicker accent, though I hadn't been around the world enough to recognize its origins.

"Very much enjoying things now that you are here," he beamed with his face shaking as he leaned in to kiss her cheek. "We are glad to have you back here, Ms. Kimberly. You have brought new associate with you, yes?"

"I have," she said without inflection. "This is Sarah Striker. She's heading strategy for Atendol."

"Ah—finally going to market—we are all so excited that Food and Drug Administration has agreed there is a need. There is a need now, right?"

We walked down a long hallway that began to decline. We were headed underground. Doors on either side of us were the only things that broke the smoothness of the walls.

"Each of those rooms has been soundproofed," Dr. Fidrych said. "We believe this gives those who work here some chances to walk down the hall and experience some of the downtime that does not exist when in the middle of an experiment. Travel time is the best time to think, no?"

What was behind those doors? How was I going to find the monkeys?

"Your ingenious proposal was forwarded to us a few days ago," the doctor said, "We've taken the liberty of moving ahead— a little, how do you say—off jump? We hope that's okay with you."

"Sure, doc," I said. "This is your world down here—I'm just trying to understand it."

He stopped short of door #455.

Kimberly was checking her beeper. Dr. Fidrych put his hand on my shoulder.

"You have signed all the necessary waivers, correct?"

When I started working at PopCore, so much of the first day was occupied with signing countless documents saying that I wouldn't report on anything that I'd seen or heard for fear that they would sue my ass and keep me in court for the rest of my life. To protect myself from such things, I always put in front of every issue of *Luddite* that the words and events that took place between its pages were entirely fictional and that any resemblance to real life was purely coincidental.

He opened the door slowly, revealing wall-to-wall couches with low lighting and music pumping in through speakers placed in each corner of the room. There were about fifteen people either lying on the floor or on the couches—all of them either making out with each other or just rubbing themselves on the thick shag carpet.

"Methylenedioxymethamphetamine," the doctor said, pronouncing each syllable with care. "We started out treating soldiers coming back from Desert Storm who might have been struggling with post-traumatic stress disorder. That one is real, by the way, in case you were wondering—at least for the soldiers coming back. Anyhow, they were given this to take the edge off their transition back to the real world.

"As you can see, if taken recreationally, the results are astounding. We had our distributors in Europe pass this out in the party scene there in the eighties and start calling it Ecstasy. The amphetamine inside is enough to create long-term attention span problems. Your plan on including it in the club scene here is spot-on—that is the correct terminology, no?"

One of the girls was alternating between rubbing herself on the edge of the leather couch and the boy passed out on the floor below her. In the corner, you could see a few of the adverse reactions taking place. Touching them seemed like it would be a bad idea.

We left the room, groans of happiness spilling everywhere behind us. I would have much rather seen the monkeys. The doctor and Kimberly were talking in whispers that I could only catch pieces of.

A group of men and women passed us in the hallway. They all had on masks and dirty hoodies covering most of their faces. One of them, a girl about the same age as me, passed by and connected with a stare. We could have been each other. They all carried backpacks and folders of papers with the words STAGE 1 written across the front. The doctor noticed me holding my eyes on them.

"We can't experiment only on animals, young lady," he said. "That wouldn't be safe for the people who really need the medication. Believe me, they are paid well for their time. They'll make five times as much in the next month than they would have in the fields picking those strawberries you eat."

A subject ran past us holding her eyes and screaming something awful.

"Eradicate this immediately!" Dr. Fidrych yelled to the attendees who were chasing down the screaming subject. "I'm sorry you have to see this." One of the attendees tackled the subject, and the others piled on.

Beneath the movement of hands trying to suppress the person, I saw the face of the girl who could have been me. Her fingernails were filthy, and the bruises on her calves looked like dark jellyfish.

"Why don't you let her go?" I said. "Is it some kind of prison?"

"She signed up for this," Kimberly said. "Once you start, it's too dangerous to get released before the trials are over. She's been in observation for too long, that's all."

"What about the bruises?" I asked. "Did they do that here?"

"That's the alternative she has to being here. Her family has probably been working farms up and down California for years. It's likely she's doing this to give them a better life."

Couldn't stand it. Started sweating. Kimberly saw me going down, put her arm around me, and walked me quickly through the hallways she knew so well until we made it outside. Doubled over and looked for a trash can to throw up in. When I found one, passed out two seconds after I saw the monkeys piled up inside.

Finding what you're looking for never looks like what you think it will.

3.

Woke up on the couch and could see the odd pairing of Alberto and Kimberly sitting at the kitchen table. Don't remember being driven home. Tried not to remember the monkeys, but they'll be with me forever now. Everything was mashing up together.

Alberto came over first with a wet towel that he laid neatly across my forehead. "What did I do to you?" he said. "We're going to stop all of this right now."

"The hell you are," I said, struggling to get up before giving in and lying back on the couch again. "We're in it now. I'm seeing this through. There's a purpose to my actions now."

Kimberly walked up behind Alberto. It wasn't until she was close up on me that I realized she was holding a copy of *Luddite*. Put my forearms over my eyes and exhaled.

"That some pretty serious stuff you're putting out there," she said. "Mind telling me why I shouldn't cut you off right now and take away your funding? Not sure you'd be able to produce the quantity like this without some serious bankroll."

I could see she'd been through the boxes stacked against the wall.

Alberto helped me up and walked with me over to the table. Guy was solid in regards to how much he loved me. He begged me not to say a word, but at this point, figured best to come as clean as I could and see what happened. Life, for me at least, is like that. You make these grand plans of how things are going to be, and though the road seems like it's unfolding before you, there's always a moment when you feel your chart isn't right. Something has gone wrong. In those moments, you need to adjust and take a chance. That's how you do something great, and goddamn it, I had come too far not to have something great come out of this. Besides, being honest had helped me move up the chain anyway, so why stop at this point?

Not sure if it was my voice or my pop's that was saying all of this, but it was coming out and coming out clear. So I spilled everything to Kimberly. Told her about how I moved out from Kansas City so that I could do it all: do my art, make some cash, live my life, and help my pops. How balancing everything wasn't too tough until I got tired or saw a trash can full of monkeys. Told her about *Luddite* and the plan for spreading the word about her industry.

You know what she wanted to hear most about?

"Tell me about your father," she said, brushing my bangs out of my face so that the towel could cool my forehead completely.

We went back and forth talking about our dads—how they were so strong in their youth and then just crumbled when they got older.

"So you're working at PopCore for him," she said.

I nodded.

"And you're doing this zine for him," she continued, nodding at Alberto.

"It started out for him," I said, sipping on some tea, "but it turned into more. Now there's a chance that all the stupid stuff I did when I was a kid, all the things that I was called a loser for, can help stop what's about to happen. It can warn people not to believe any of this crap that's being put out. Not the Internet, not the medications, not the doctors that are preaching. And if I lose? Well, at least I go down knowing I followed the righteous path. What are you going to tell yourself when the money isn't enough for you?"

Her eyes had filled with water, and then they gave. Her makeup smeared, and she started bawling. Not what I expected, but it was moving, nonetheless. She curled up next to me, and we held each other through the night.

Alberto went back to the table and continued stapling issues of *Luddite*.

CHAPTER 15

1.

Being back at the old house on McAllister gave me a few flash-backs. Remembered Josephine and how she looked on her first day of moving in—how she just wanted a place to crash out and recover from the pain that she'd caused and then had been caused to her.

Victor came out quick and invited me inside, but I had no interest in making small talk. We knew what was up. Handed him a JanSport backpack with silver paint marker graffiti all over it. Colin had stayed up all night designing that thing.

"Now look, Victor," I said, leveling eyes with him. "There's two bags in there. One of them is for you, so you don't go and pinch from the others. Be sure you get it all out in the club tonight. Once you're empty, we'll refill you. It's not going to be me who's coming by. We've got others for that. Cool with you?"

He grabbed the bag and nodded.

"After you get your customer base," I continued, "you can start laying it off on others. Make sure they aren't at the same clubs. Have them dress the same when they're selling. Use the word Ecstasy as much as you can. Tell your other sellers to do the same."

"Thanks for thinking of me on this," he said. "It's going to be my ticket to being part of something. Much appreciated."

"No worries." I smiled. "Just make sure I get my forty per-cent. We'll be good as long as that happens."

Of course I was going to cut myself in on some side profits. Shaden Healthcare wrote it off as an operating expense. Cleaning all of that cash was going to be too much of a pain for them. For me, I just used that as my spending money to live on around the city and had my legitimate checks direct-deposited into an account I had set up for my pops back in KC.

He closed the door, and I had spun around to leave when our old door opened up again. Valerie was standing in the doorway, talking on a phone connected to a long cord that reached all the way back upstairs.

She didn't say a word to me—just picked up the newspaper from the stoop, kept on talking with whoever she was talking to on the phone, walked back upstairs, and left the door open for me if I wanted to follow or not.

Walked slowly up the stairs after her. It felt cleaner. Less dust. The wood on the staircase had been polished so the carved-out workmanship was now fully on display. Reaching the living room, I saw that everything had been redone. New floors. A new stereo.

Valerie was on the phone drumming up business. "So we're going to do it this Friday, here, okay," she said. "I'm going to need proper lighting this time, and make sure everything is catered. Can't have people leaving because they're hungry. Yes. Great. Thanks."

She hung up the phone and looked at me. Looked fantastic. Glowing.

"Hear that silence." She beamed. "It's all mine. Kicked everyone out, including the junk, and now I'm living clean. Turned this place into a righteous dungeon and making plenty of loot. Things are looking up."

"You're not dancing anymore?" I asked, moving a little further in to see the work she'd had done to the kitchen.

"I'm only working for myself, lady. Pulling in cash for others is for suckers. Don't feel bad, though—it takes a little while to realize that for yourself. How are things with you two?"

"We're not a two," I answered. "We just doing this stretch of life together."

I hardly recognized the person across from me. She had built herself back from a shell and gotten rid of everyone who had been feeding off her.

"You should come by for one of the shows," she said. "It's a good time for everyone involved, that's for sure. Haven't gotten any write-ups yet, but word is spreading. Word spreads, you know. You might do an issue about me."

The phone rang again, and she didn't hesitate to answer it. Pulled out a datebook and started checking what dates she had open. There were a few items that I had wanted to grab from my room upstairs, but before asking, I knew they were all probably gone. Even if they weren't, I didn't need them anymore. Smiled and nodded at her, and she halfway returned the gesture.

Walked down the stairs with the now perfectly polished handrails and back into the city.

Down McAllister and out to Fillmore. Down again. Down past Haight Street, where protesters were carrying picket signs around the housing projects and yelling at the bulldozers that were readying themselves to erase the affordable housing in the name of cool loft space.

Down to the N Judah Line by the Safeway, where I stopped for a moment to watch the line turn slowly and descend into the tunnels like a python. As it moved down and away, it revealed Colin standing and looking into the tunnel, both hands holding the straps of his backpack.

Rolled up to him, but he kept his eyes looking down the tunnel, then up and around.

"You look like you're casing the place for a hit or something," I said. "What gives?"

"Who talks like that anymore?" he answered. "Why can't you just say what you want to say? Nobody says what they want to anymore."

My head dropped a bit, and I looked for something to kick up.

"Sorry. I had to get away from that damn computer," he said, moving closer to the tunnel. "Haven't been able to keep a thought in my head more than a minute. Usually I can spend hours on a sketch, but I'm jumping from piece to piece these days. Losing it. Maybe I have the ADD."

Felt it, too. Was speaking in quick sentences and not finishing thoughts. We were creating the symptoms outside of the lab and in the real world, but it had to be rubbing off on us as well.

Colin looked deep into the tunnel. Cans of Krylon jingled inside his backpack.

"Never been down in the tunnels before," I said to break the thickness. "Only seen it go by real quick from inside the train. Closest I've come to being inside one of those things is watching *Style Wars* with Fred Mason over at his house when his father would pass out and I'd let him put his hand down my shirt if he let me borrow his records. His brother was in school in New York, so he would send home all of these albums and videos. Remember the first time I heard 'Criminal Minded'—oh man, almost lost my mind."

> *Criminal minded, you've been blinded, looking for style like this, you can't find it. They are the audience, I am the lyricist.*
>
> —*Boogie Down Productions*

"Eric B. and Rakim soon after that. Must have listened to 'Chinese Arithmetic' for a month straight."

Colin smiled at that.

"Tonight we go," he said. "You shouldn't just experience things through movies."

2.

It's 12:55 a.m. and the last N Judah rolls out. After that, the trains close down and the buses turn to Night Owls. The underground becomes silent. Walked through the tunnels without the light of expectations shining on me. Nice to follow someone else. Colin had gotten an old miner's hat at a thrift store in the Castro just for this evening, and he was wearing one of those photographer's vests with a million pockets all over the place.

You could see what he was looking at with each turn of his head. Instructions on what to do with the rails on the tracks didn't need to be told. After all, I had seen *Beat Street* a million times—remember yelling at the TV telling Ramo not to chase Spit through the tunnels. Still remember his pops looking at the White Whale he finally tagged when the elevated train ran through the end of the movie.

Those are our scriptures. Our captures of a time that was not meant to be captured but lived. We exist on that foundation. Through the tunnels retracing steps of masters who never thought there were going to be masters.

Colin settled on a spot that was faded enough to go over. He reached into his backpack and brought out his sketchbook. Twenty pages dedicated to this one piece. Maps and speeds of when and how fast the trains went by. Everything planned out so that when he did what he was there to do, it would be seen.

"Doesn't matter how many people see it," he said. "Only the people that need to see it. Some do, and some don't. That's that. No?"

Out with the cans. Had my Canon AE1 with me, and I held it up to him as if to ask if he minded that I document what was happening. He seemed cool with everything.

Thing about a roll of film is you need to be selective on what you decide to take.

Filler first. Light. Just for shape. Then outline. Quick. There was no time for contemplation. That was all done behind the scenes. Whole throw-up was done in about three minutes. He put the cans back in his pack and turned around.

"Damian," he said. "Straight Damian."

"What are you talking about?"

"The mark. Left my mark so they know who was part of it."

We walked back through the tunnel in silence, the light on his miner's hat illuminating the work of others who had come before.

Right when we made it to the mouth of the tunnel, flashing lights bounced on us. Colin recognized the cops right away. He looked me in the eye, motioned left, and then took off that way down towards Market Street. Broke with him. The cop chasing us wore that heavy SF uniform and was breathing heavy under his mustache.

"I'll shoot!" he screamed. "Stop running away from me!"

Each stride we took distanced us. Cops in SF were out of shape and heavy smokers. No way he would be able to hang. Down across Market Street not looking at the cars crossing. Cop couldn't make it across the river. Didn't even draw his gun.

We kept going a few more blocks up and didn't stop until we reached the Castro. Two old men in white suits strolled holding hands, swinging back and forth. Nice to see people in love. Colin swung his backpack around and checked to make sure nothing had fallen out.

A bus pulled up silently, and he jumped through the back doors. Let them close and let him go. In and out of lives we moved back then, without regard to what that meant. He leaned back and became one of the faces going into the night. Could see him tagging up the inside window as it passed away.

Castro never quieted down, even at this time of night. Remember wishing for the theater to be open so I could watch the man who played the piano before the show walk with his wife up the aisle while everyone applauded. Last time I was there they were showing a double feature of *The Wild Bunch* and *The Magnificent Seven*. Everyone was going crazy that night.

But this was this night. Down Castro I went—past the bondage stores, one of which might have been the camera shop where Harvey Milk started out. Stopped at Escape from New York Pizza where I could get a slice of pesto and just post up by the window and look out at the world passing by. In Kansas City it would have been the same people passing by on a loop, but here, it was everyone who had left those towns to make up the endless displays of folks moving around in front of me.

Started thinking about the next issue and how I would put those pictures of Colin in there. *The Mark Issue.* Eating a slice of pizza in the late-night hours of San Francisco by yourself is a moment that is oftentimes looked over and added to the countless frames of life without realizing the importance of pausing. Settled on one thought as much as I could and tried to hold it. So difficult to do. The people behind the counter mixed dough and took orders. The city needed to be fed.

3.

Back at the office. The community that the empty space created was starting to bother a few of the developers and writers, so cubicles had been constructed to give the illusion of privacy. Had stacks of papers and reports everywhere that I tried like hell to put into notebooks, but they were insisting that I use a computer and just e-mail everything.

Soon, nobody was leaving their cubicles to talk anymore, and we were either e-mailing each other random thoughts or scheduling meetings, or speaking over an instant message chat.

Now we only heard our own voices as we typed up and hit send.

You could hear the clicking coming over the thin walls of the cubes, so people started wearing headphones. Can you imagine that? An office where everyone is wearing headphones and not speaking with each other?

The cubicle walls made the space we had for our desks seem all the smaller.

Most of my days were focused on finding out ways to spread the word how the Internet and Ecstasy were causing the youth of America to develop ADD, while my nights were spent putting together issues of *Luddite* exposing what I was doing in the daytime.

Alberto met me outside the office to say hello and throw me a lifeline from outside the corporate world. Make no mistake that, even though we were in a warehouse, it was still the corporate world. If I've learned anything from that experience it's that corporations do their best not to make themselves look corporate. They know. They do.

Alberto looked in decent shape. He'd just come from laying *Luddite* all around the city. Big smile on his face.

"People were waiting for me this time," he said. "They knew what I was carrying. Amazing. We're doing it!"

He tried to kiss me, but I backed away—not wanting anyone to see what I was connected to. Bad enough Kimberly had found us out, and she hadn't made an appearance since that night. Was a little bit paranoid. She could have gone either way, and at that point I didn't have enough money saved to save my pop.

Was about to disappear around the corner when Belt stepped out and called after me.

"Sarah, we need you inside," he said. "Sorry to interrupt your plans."

Felt Alberto's hand slip out of mine.

"Can't it wait?" I said. "I've got—"

But then it was Alberto who gave in. It was he who gave me back over.

He leaned in.

"We're too close now," he told me. "There's time for lunches later."

Right there I knew he was nothing like my father. That man never missed one night at the table with my grilled cheese sandwiches, no matter how tired he was or where his mind drifted. Hell, the guy was probably dying of cancer for a good portion of those lunches, and here was this guy handing me back into the corporate world.

Good. That was fine. Without Alberto I wouldn't be where I was. I'd still be chasing indie-rock girls around the city instead of exposing these people out here trying to make money off of the sickness they cause us.

There were more people in the office each week. Younger by the day. Typing away and looking into the screen. Eyes were drooping. Many of us were working thirteen-hour days, six days a week.

The fact that we could wear T-shirts and jeans into the office was no longer a novelty. Think it was starting to get to everyone there. Thing is, in the older days, you'd have to dress up for the office, and though you'd be uncomfortable, there was that moment after work when you'd come home and remove your clothes and feel the restrictions lift away. Men untied their ties and walked around in their undershirts, while women undid their stockings and un-tucked whatever they might have tucked in.

"We're testing faster connections," said Anton Fleece, the lead IT guy in the office. "I got awarded a beta tester position with Wireless World Technology. We'll be receiving many other inventions because of this. There is very much a need to thank me."

IT guys said whatever they wanted because they knew nobody could do what they did. He skated away on his old Aaron Murray original, going to find the next person he could tell.

All of those commercials in the eighties telling you that there was no need for college if you went to one of these technical schools that taught you how to code and fix computers were laughed at, mocked. Never had the choice myself, but if I had, I would have still chosen college and dorms over the dark rooms of technical computer-building schools.

Now these people had all the power. They controlled the communication lines. We were able to jump from website to website with greater ease. The amount of information available to us was astounding. New sites were popping up from everywhere. Each company had one. Every person registered their name. New islands of humanity were being carved out right in front of us all.

Identity and time were becoming digital. The amount of time needed to walk down those blocks to find something unique was melting away. We were told to bring our uniqueness into the fold and give it away.

Days were spent, and billed, at websites created by teens with new blog-creating platforms to see what they were writing about, how short their sentences were, and where they were linking to. Pretty sure that we had created those blogging sites so that these kids would just put out there what we needed to know.

We'd target them with websites and articles talking about ADD and send them press releases with information about the new diseases. Time became irrelevant with how much time we were spending on the computer. How long had I been in San Francisco? How long since I talked to my father? Couldn't keep anything right in my head. There were soda bottles everywhere. New espresso machines made us wound up and ready to pounce.

Anton was skating back and forth helping out those who couldn't figure out their computers. Out of the corner of my eye, I spotted Kimberly walking out of the office struggling to hold her folder and her purse at the same time while still walking with her distinct strut.

Slunk down a bit in my chair trying to avoid being seen.

"You're trying to avoid me," she said, walking over. "There's no need for that."

She sat on my desk and crossed her legs, then looked around to see if anyone was watching her before she pulled a copy of *Luddite* out of her purse.

"It's incredible," she said softly. "The pictures you find that seem to be random always go perfectly with the story. I devoured every word. Now, I can't say that I believed everything I read, but that's more about the person I am than what you're saying here. Don't stop this. In fact, I want to help you. Is that alright?"

"I was getting ready to pack my desk," I told her. "How can you want me to make something that goes against what you stand for?"

"Girl," she said, leaning back a little bit so I could see the space that opened up a bit between her blouse buttons, "this is my job, not who I am. Besides, what I enjoy most is seeing creations brought to life. You're doing that. I'm not sure what you're up to is going to stop the sales of the drugs, but it's going to do something. I'd like to see what it does. I'd also like to see you succeed."

She smiled and put an envelope on my desk with my name written in perfect penwomanship.

Opened it up and found a check for ten grand.

Funny thing about getting something that big in your hands for the first time, especially if you've been poor most of your life. Especially if you've ever had to put together change in order to eat. Was making enough on my own to put this right in the mail to my pops.

Gave me a warm feeling to be doing so, but something else was tugging. Why was Kimberly not going to blow me out of the water for trying to bring down the company? Maybe she didn't think I could. Maybe she didn't care either way. No idea. She was into it. Made me think of all the people that Valerie used to get paid to beat down. Maybe inside Kimberly really wanted to be beaten down for putting all that poison into the world and creating diseases.

Could hear my pops from the kitchen table come in like a scratch from Eric B.: "Be wary of people who go out of their way in charity. They're usually compensating for some evil they're trying to erase."

The high-speed connection that was available now had me searching through site after site in record time. Stayed for about two minutes on each, though I couldn't keep track of minutes. Seconds. Hours. Kept jumping to the next and jotting down notes. Back and forth from my notepad to the document I had open on the computer. Each time I went to write using the computer, I opened up another website. Couldn't stop. No focus. Nothing. Thousands of voices all strung together reaching across the country from small towns in Wisconsin to Rochester, Minnesota, where I found a website by this girl who didn't have many friends but liked to visit the local thrift store and buy used books and records.

Made me stop for a moment and get up. Had found myself out there. Found that there were many of me and my uniqueness was not mine. It was a connection that jolted me. Ran for some quarters from the laundry around the corner and then ran to the payphone. Dialed. Mom again. Pop asleep. Exhausted, she said. The money I'd been sending was doing a world of good. Told her I had plenty. Keep sending, she said. Stop working, Mom. No response. Just more about Pops. Wanted to speak with him in the worst way. Next week give it a try.

Back to work and online for hours.

4.

Made my way upstairs and unlocked the door expecting to see Alberto there cooking up some meal and preaching to me about the next steps in our grand plans for the city.

There were stacks of *Luddite* everywhere, but no Alberto. Couldn't understand it. Usually if he was gone there'd be a note or something. Thought of Kimberly and wondered if I could see myself finally settle into a life of just one person. Kids. House. Growing old. All of the things that had been in front of me but were beyond my reach. My bank account was full. Was doing something with my life.

Could hear the silence that takes over San Francisco. Wished train whistles were going off in my head to feel at home. Never quite did here.

The big launch was going to be coming up soon. Turned on the news and saw an exposé telling parents about this new drug called Ecstasy and how kids are gathering at parties to take this pill.

"The effects of this on children at such a young age can include loss of memory and the onset of attention deficit disorder, better known as ADD."

Our copywriters were amazing.

Getting that on the air and in front of parents was the thing that needed to be done. We had done our job, and in a big way. Word had to be spreading across the country about this. Home labs around the country were opening up now producing Ecstasy because everyone wanted to be part of the new scene we'd created.

We had drugged the country so that we could drug the country.

Alberto walked in the door drunk. He couldn't make eye contact with me. Tossed down the bag he had been biking around the city with and lay flat on the couch.

"Are you ever going to love me?" he said. "I think I have a right to know."

"What do you want me to tell you?" I whispered. "I wish I felt the same love you do."

"I can't just keep looking at you every day," he told me. "It needs to be more or I have to leave. I'm dying inside. No matter what we accomplish during the day, if I can't be with you fully at night, if you can't give yourself to me in every way, it's torture for me."

"You're going to leave me? What about our plans? We have to keep going!"

He rolled over and was on the verge of passing out.

"At this point, I'm just a delivery boy. You're doing it all on your own. No doubt you can find someone with a larger distribution ability than me. Shouldn't be too hard with your new partner."

He motioned towards the check on the table before continuing.

"She's just looking at it from a research perspective. Couldn't care less about what happens either way. Just a game to her."

He focused what he had left inside of him.

"She's got more game than you can handle," he said. "You think she's funding you? You think she wants you to succeed?"

"No," I said. "But I can move around her. I've been inside long enough."

"That's the problem," he said. "You're on the inside."

CHAPTER 16

i.

We started running the reports in early summer of '95, and soon after, the sales of Atendol started to ignite. Parents were afraid their kids were developing ADD because of the parties they were going to, or because of the time spent in front of video games, or the newly bursting computer fad. Is the Internet causing ADD? Those reports were all Golden Grahams for us.

Even the kids themselves enjoyed saying it. It was that double D in ADD that caused the tongue to bounce off the roof of the mouth. Gave a nice feeling. Parents and teens were going to the doctor in record numbers to ask for any medication that could treat ADD. Of course, we'd planned the awareness campaign so far in advance that when the news started to spread about the disease, we had the only drug on the market. Reps were waiting in offices with short skirts and heavy bags of samples to give the doc so when the doc had people coming in asking for a cure for ADD, well, what else were they going to give them?

To educate the doctors, we had to create these things called vis aids (visual aids). These are what the reps took out into the field with them to show the doctor in their five minutes of face time—explaining the disease and what to look for in their patients who might be coming in. Digital versions of these were leaked to the patient population so that they could educate themselves in what they believed to be the scientific explanation of ADD.

If you really want to market medicine to consumers, the best method is to have them believe they've discovered it themselves.

Usually targeted things like "trigger words"—words patients would say when speaking to their doc about what's bothering them.

Doctor, I can't focus. Hey, Doc, I can't concentrate at work. Can't even complete a newspaper article. Focus. Concentrate. Complete.

All of these words pointed us towards something called the indications. See, pharmacy companies can't get in there and just say whatever they want. They need to make sure that doctors are only prescribing it to treat what the FDA says it can.

All the clinical trials we performed generated data that we submitted to the FDA, where they vote on whether or not a drug can be used for an indication. So, let's say you have a drug like ours. Doctors can prescribe it only for ADD because it received that indication. When you see the words "indicated for so and so," that means doctors can only prescribe it for that specific thing.

Meaning, if you came in and said, "Doc, I have this crazy headache, but I need to work. Do you have anything?" they couldn't prescribe you Atendol for headaches. But if you said that you were having trouble *concentrating*, well then, you might get it. See—trigger words. This way, when you start to develop that rash underneath your eyelids that 6.73 percent of the people in the clinical trials did and think about suing your doctor, they can point to the "Important Safety Information" and say you were warned when they prescribed it for your ADD.

Cool, huh? Pharmaceutical companies know they are going to get sued—they have that budgeted out—but they don't like it. So every time you put out any piece of advertising, you need to take it through something called a med/legal review.

These are kind of awesome and where we were headed when they finished the website for Atendol.

Now, these reviews were amazing in the way they illuminated the lunacy of the people in charge. See, Shaden Healthcare kept doctors and lawyers on staff at salaries that would astonish you.

Tim drove with me up to the med/legal review at Shaden. Tim was a cool enough guy when you spoke to him. Could go either way on any subject and was a big sports nut and a huge Giants fan who loved going out to Candlestick Park even when it got windy and nobody else was in the stands to cheer. Thought when I met him my pops would have liked him because he seemed genuine and had a beard.

Seeing that glass building again, how clean it was from the outside, jolted me inside, but I put myself together and tried to focus on the three secretaries who sat in a line answering phones, not what I knew existed in the trash cans outside.

Tim and I walked through the door talking about whether the third PE album held weight against the second when Audrey stepped in the middle of our conversation and grabbed Tim's arm.

Kid shrunk right there.

She was a mess and stressed out—her horse-face moving in a million directions. Her low-cut blouse showed off her hideous boobs that were so much in Tim's face that no matter where he tried to look, she swung around to make sure she, they, were in his line of sight.

She talked a mile a minute and kept her head on a constant swivel to see who was listening to her or see what she could hear. She didn't acknowledge me and pulled Tim aside and stared talking softly into his ear. Could see her moving up against him so that she'd rub once in a while. He winced, but didn't pull back.

They broke and started heading toward the elevator. He motioned for me to follow them in, then positioned me in the middle so he could have a break from her advances. Door opened and he shot out, but she nudged me out of the way and went right behind him. Went by her desk and saw the little, unspectacular cubicle and could see right there why she was so upset. The walls around her were this odd shade of half beige, half orange.

People hunched over antiquated computers with faded pieces of paper they thought were important enough at one time to put up on their makeshift walls.

Into the room with the long table. Audrey situated herself next to Tim. I sat as far away as possible with the printout of all the webpages in front of me. Two men sat on either side of the middle of the table facing each other—each battling to see who would be the first to bust a pants button from too many trips to the company vending machines. A slim girl sat at the head of the table with copies of the printouts all ready. Small talk was taking place about how the traffic was and what they'd seen on TV the night before. The two men at the center of the table never introduced themselves, but Tim told me before to expect one doctor and one lawyer to be running the show.

Can't tell you their names because I don't remember, and to tell you the truth, the only way I could tell them apart was from the titles that they held. The doctor asked if anyone had seen the episode of *Seinfeld* the night before.

Kimberly walked in finishing up a phone call. All three men in the room stopped what they were doing for a second and were captivated by her. Audrey's shoulders slumped like that kid who never got picked for a kickball game.

Kimberly sat down next to me, leaned in, and explained who was who.

"Even if they say something that doesn't make sense," she whispered, "don't argue. Just write it down and make whatever changes they ask for. Their job is to make sure we don't say anything that's not proven."

"Nobody saw it?" the doctor said, and then he started his reenactment of the show. "Well George falls for this woman and says…" The doctor went on for about five minutes talking about the damn episode, pausing only to laugh at his own recollection, which Audrey mirrored with a laugh, which was then followed by a chuckle from Tim.

People reciting TV episodes before reviewing documents that will convince consumers to take a pill that will in all likelihood give them some form of medical defect. Nice. These are the people controlling the healthcare industry.

Tim's leg was shaking under the table while Audrey talked to him and searched for reasons to touch him wherever she could. The slim moderator at the head of the table cleared her throat and began the med/legal review. On the front page of the site, we had two pictures: one of a wild-eyed dog, the other of a sleeping kitten. The thought of course being that you'd become calmer if you took Atendol.

"Well, I'm not sure you can show this," the lawyer said, "because it implies that if you take this, then your ability to sleep is going to increase. We can't make that claim."

"True," the doctor said, nodding. "You're not concentrating when you're sleeping. Why not show a child sitting calmly in a classroom raising his or her hand?"

"Well," the lawyer interrupted, "you wouldn't show them raising their hands because that would imply that your child is going to be smarter if they take this. Perhaps we can show them just paying attention."

Nobody said a word. Everyone nodded.

The moderator made the notes and continued on. We all made the notes and continued on. It went like that for hours.

The claim that we could make when speaking of Atendol was:

> Atendol is approved for the treatment of ADD (attention deficit disorder) in conjunction with counseling and other therapies approved by your doctor. Atendol is known to control the symptoms of ADD but does not control the ADD itself.

Right. So you have to notice two things right there. First, it does not treat the disorder, which isn't real anyway. It only treats the *symptoms*. Second, the pill alone is not going to control the symptoms.

The clinical trials that had been running for the past two years were used as the backbone for papers written by doctors hired by us, and these were used as references to back up any claims we might have made on the website. It was a tedious task to listen to the doctor and lawyer go back and forth, earning their four hundred dollars an hour to make sure everything was safe from lawsuits, while, at the same time, making sure their jobs meant enough to keep them on payroll.

Tim never said a word to protest any of their comments, while Audrey would say something just to say something, only to back down and tell the doctor and lawyer they were right. She'd laugh and jiggle her horrible breasts, which to them, after sitting in their beige offices all day long waiting for the next check to be direct-deposited into their bank accounts, must have looked good enough to think about later.

It was over and I was ready to break out of there. Tried to get Tim to roll quickly with me so we could get back to the city and enjoy at least some part of the day. They had made so many changes to the website copy and art that the work ahead was pretty significant for the team waiting on those comments. Now, that's not necessarily a bad thing because it gave us more time and more money in the budget. After all, the client has to pay more cash if the med/legal review board makes changes that are outside the original statement of work (that's SOW).

Just as Tim was getting ready to join me, Audrey tapped him on the shoulder and asked him to go with her to do a recap of the meeting.

"You can wait in the lobby," she said without looking at me. The first words she had spoken to me that day.

Went out into the lobby to see if I could get a smile from one of the three receptionists. MOA videos played all around us. MOA stands for "mechanism of action," which shows exactly how the drug may be working inside the body. You always have to say "may be" or "might be," because you can never flat-out say that something these companies make actually works.

Watched the loops of the science videos and thought about how valid any of them were. What was being taught was being created. My eyes were getting tired processing all of the information. Everything was so clean out here in front. Tried to focus my eyes on one thing, but kept shooting all over the place. Couldn't hold a thought.

Tim walked out from behind the doors and looked a little out of sorts, but he was odd, anyhow, so I didn't pay it any mind.

"We ready to get out of here?" I asked.

"What?" he said. "We should get out of here. You ready?"

"That's what I just asked. You okay?"

He smelled the tops of his fingers, made a sickened kind of face, and then just walked out the door to the parking lot. Once we got into the car, I could smell it too. Something rotten. Looked at the bottom of my shoes, afraid I had stepped in something. Tim tried not to notice me looking for the cause of the smell. It wasn't me. He realized I realized that. He started the engine and drove his way out of the lot, looking ashamed and never again in my eyes.

"How could you do that?" I asked. "She's a monster."

"Living the dream," he said. "It is what it is."

He reached over and pulled a wet nap out of the glove box and attempted to wipe himself clean. We drove back to the city in silence, but inside he must have been screaming. What did he do with all of that rage? Perhaps that's why people like Valerie existed.

CHAPTER 17

i.

"You're getting promoted," Belt said. "I need someone to lead who can deal with the clients and doesn't mind traveling once in a while. You up for it?"

"Sure," I said, surprised and not knowing if I should accept or not. "What exactly am I being promoted to?"

"You're going to be VP of Digital Strategy and Development. Talking to new companies. Finding the most efficient methods to build awareness campaigns. Getting products in front of the youth market. You're up for it. I think so. Hell, even Kimberly feels like you should be heading this."

"Kimberly?"

"Yep. Met with her last night over a few drinks. That woman can put them away. She thinks you're something. Said I better promote you or I might lose you. So, you're up and in. Your salary jumps to a hundred thousand a year plus bonuses for accounts you bring in. How's that sound?"

"Sounds ridiculous," I told him. "But not like anything I could think of turning down."

"Just don't leave me," he said. "I need you in the package."

He went on to his computer and forgot about me. Back at my desk, there was an e-mail waiting for me from Kimberly.

Sarah,

I'm in love with you. Don't care if you feel the same way or not. Let me take you out tonight and we'll decide then. I'm waiting outside now. Don't worry about walking out on anyone. You're in charge. No need to sit in front of the computer any longer.

—Kimberly

Was tired of thinking and planning things out. Got up from my desk and walked out into the strangely sunny San Francisco day. Kimberly was outside sitting in the driver's seat of a convertible Volkswagen Rabbit that she had redone and chromed out. So cool.

Jumped in the front seat.

She put her hand gently on my knee and dropped her sunglasses down.

"Hope you don't mind about pushing you for the promotion," she said. "That I did because you deserve it. Today I want to do because *I* deserve it."

Away we went. Out of the warehouse district and over the Golden Gate Bridge. It was the first time since I'd lived in the city that I had driven over it. There had never been any reason to go over to Marin County. Alberto was from there but never wanted to go home. Guess that was one thing we both had in common.

As we started over the bridge, we passed over old army forts that were built during the Civil War and reused in WWII when there was the threat of being attacked by sea again. Cannons and gun turrets, though abandoned, still line the outskirts of San Francisco. Perhaps the ghosts are keeping watch to make sure nobody sneaks in overnight.

The sun stayed out as we continued across the bridge. It was one of those rare days when you could see the entire city and bay backed by perfect blue. Anyone who had any sense at all was escaping from their offices and going to lie on a piece of grass somewhere.

Kimberly pushed in the tape and let Digable Planets play us out of the city.

Through Marin, you enter tunnels with rainbows painted over the arches. We passed over Sausalito without stopping.

"We'll stop by on the way back," Kimberly said. "I want to go rock-picking with you."

We turned off and went through the hills of Marin until we were on a road in the woods that eventually spat us out to the ocean. The surf outside was round and pounding against itself. The wind ripped over the car. Could barely hear the music, much less Kimberly.

Was about to take my shoes off when she stopped me.

"Take a close look," she said.

Leaned out the window and saw that the sand of the beach was actually made up of these tiny pebbles. They stretched out forever. There was no sand at all.

"That's amazing," I told her. "Glad I brought my camera. Oh wait!"

Reached into my bag and found an empty film canister.

We walked out to the beach, sat down in the middle of the pebbles, and began searching through them for rare colors and smooth shapes. None of the pebbles could have been bigger that a quarter of my fingernail.

"Such a relief looking at something natural," I told her. "Looking into a computer screen all day is painful deep inside my brain. Know what I mean?"

"How about we don't talk about work at all?" she said. "Nothing about changing the world. Nothing about what we're going to do. Only what's happening now. At this moment."

"And what's that?" I asked, moving my finger over her eyelid and feeling a layer of salt that had made its way up from the sea. "What's happening now?"

We left it unanswered and spent the next few hours collecting pebbles and dropping them into the film canister. Once in a while, our fingers would rub against each other as we moved from the surface of the pebbles.

No idea where any of them came from or why they had yet to be broken down into indistinguishable sand.

"I used to come here as a kid," she said, looking out over the horizon. "Only thing in my life that has stayed exactly the same. Even that log over there. The one with the tire around it. My brother and I used to try like crazy to get that tire to come off, but it never would. We'd spend our whole day trying to rip that thing off. No doubt thousands of other kids tried the same thing. Nobody ever could."

"How'd it get on there in the first place?" I asked.

Kim leaned in and kissed me. Her tongue was so clean-tasting. Lips just right against the weight of mine. It was like a kiss between fifteen-year-olds, when everything was put into it and it wasn't just a first step in a longer process.

We kissed on the pebbles until the sun went down with her childhood memories singing like a chorus in the background shadows.

2.

Lying on my couch, all I could think about was when I would see Kimberly again. It was the most away from myself I'd ever felt. Alberto had moved out and left the apartment for me. Said he couldn't be alone in it after we had been together.

Doorbell.

Alberto. He looked good. Think that happens to people after you haven't seen them for a while. They lose that familiarity of being seen every day. He picked up the latest batch of *Luddite: The Medical Review Issue* and stopped before he went out the door. He looked at me and then, in his eyes, the way he was into me, I could tell that I was in love with Kimberly because I understood, finally, how it looked in reflection.

"I started my own messenger service," he said. "Figured everyone else was going out of business, so it was smart to be the only one. It can't go completely digital yet. There's got to be a need. Besides, what else am I going to do? You holding up okay in there?"

Sometimes I forgot I was undercover until Alberto reminded me I was living two lives.

"I'm fine," I told him. "The stuff I'm seeing, though, it's tough to forget. Tough to get to sleep at night."

"You shouldn't forget about any of it," he said. "But sleeping at night, being able to live with yourself, shouldn't be a problem. You're doing something about it."

Couldn't really tell if he was right or not. Was I fighting it or making money off of the problem itself and making a name for myself for fighting it? Lived with the conflict, as I think these things, these run-ups against each other, exist in everyone. There is no linear life.

"Hey," I said as he was about to leave. "Thought you were going to have someone else pick those up and deliver them around. Glad you decided otherwise."

"Don't be a sap," he said before breaking out into a rare smile that fought to find room on his face. "I expect to well paid by this well-off executive. Trickle it down, baby!"

We both laughed and shared that moment.

He looked around and saw how I was living. Still saw the ramen packages everywhere.

"You can keep a little of it for yourself," he said. "Don't think a few hundred here and there would make that much of a difference."

"You never know which dollar it's going to be that makes the difference," I replied. "Besides, I don't mind not living it up on the dollars I'm pulling in."

"Most?"

"Don't make me explain," I told him. "Just enjoy how much you've helped. It's rare."

He walked out with his stack of deliveries.

3.

Everyone was munching through a good spread of food, gathered in the main conference room, when I got to work. Wasn't hungry myself, as Kimberly and I met early and had coffee and bagels at the Bohemian Cigar Store café in North Beach. She had gotten there early to make sure we had two seats at the counter.

Could still feel her kisses as I walked into the meeting. Belt was standing next to a man in slacks, who was rolling up the sleeves of his dress shirt to try and fit in a little more. Belt waved me over.

"What's going on?" I asked.

"You're about to find out," he said. "It's good for you though. More cash. More responsibility. Greater exposure."

He smiled and walked towards a microphone that had been set up for him. In his voice and movements, I could tell he thought he was doing the right thing.

Clearing his throat.

"Okay everyone," he started in. "You know I've always given you news without a filter. Today is no different. Today, the work we have done over the last two years has paid off. The results you have generated have allowed us to take this operation to the next level—but for me, this is where I move on.

"I leave you in the hands of one of the great agencies in the game. The people of FHB are responsible for first putting toys in cereal boxes, the first to make chewable vitamins with cartoon characters on them, and now, the first to buy a digital agency to be part of their main group. Integration. I give you Monty Freeman."

Everyone clapped sporadically, but you could tell nobody knew what they were clapping for.

Monty stepped forward, but not before chugging half a cup of coffee, which could be heard over the mic. He popped in a piece of hard candy just before he spoke and moved it around every ten seconds or so.

"So, you're wondering who I am and why this guy standing here is my next boss. Don't worry. I've been many people's bosses over the last twenty years, but not in this digital game. But let's face it, advertising is advertising, and I know advertising.

"Over the next few days, I'll be here just kind of looking around and seeing what you're all up to and watching your process. Then I can see how your process is going to be our process, and how we can work synergistically together to make the transition work for everyone. Of course, some of you may choose that it's not right for you, and that's fine. You need to make the moves that are best for you. But those of you who do decide to move on with us, you'll find the experience to be enlightening. We're going to be moving fast, and that's my style. I'm here to make things move.

"Now, I know you all have some questions, but there's not enough time to answer all of them here. My office is going to be open to all of you, as soon as I meet with the top-level execs, and then I would be glad to answer any questions you might have left over. Okay? Okay."

He walked away from the microphone and finished the other half of his coffee during his retreat into his office.

Looked at Belt, who was having a little trouble looking me in the eyes.

"You sold the company?" I asked. "How could you do that? Thought this was your child. Your baby."

"Twenty-five million dollars they gave me," he said. "I'm into it about seven. That's an amazing profit margin and was in the plans all along. You're going to make out fine, though. A few deals were put in place so that the people who are key to running and making this all go stay in place. You need to stay in place. You actually helped close the sale."

"How's that?" I asked, my head still spinning. "What could I have done to close the sale?"

"Well, the company is made up of people and perceived value. We put everyone onto a balance sheet, laid out their salaries, then laid out how much they actually brought in. You're worth *a lot* more than we pay you, even with the raise!"

He laughed but pulled it in when he saw that I wasn't laughing.

"You sold us all," I said, a little in disbelief, though not surprised, at how quickly human lives could be put into an Excel spreadsheet under the heading "Commodity." "That's revolting."

"No more revolting than selling medications you know don't work," he leaned in and whispered. "No more revolting than knowingly doing experiments on people. Besides, not everyone was 'sold.' Not everyone was valuable enough to be sold. Don't be so self-righteous. We're all participating in this game. Doesn't matter your level of participation. If you know, and you're in, then you know. Besides, you have your own agenda, right?"

He turned and walked away, but before I could call after him, I smelled the mix of coffee and Now and Laters behind me.

"Want you to come into my office for a minute," Monty said. "Word is you're the person I should talk to. Don't worry about Belt over there, he's happy to be on his way out. Probably bought himself a spot on an island somewhere he thinks he'll be happy at. That's not us though, is it?"

He'd called us an *us*, which was a little disturbing. The guy was licking his lips, looking for another cup of coffee, while we walked into his office. Called the girl who was at the front desk and about to become his assistant and asked her to bring him in a cup of coffee and a box of bottled water.

"Sit, sit," he said, unscrewing the cap of a bottle and drinking it down on his way into the chair. "You were the most talked-about person during negotiations, or so I hear—that's above my pay grade to know the details. Anyway: I need someone to take control of this next campaign, and I think you should be doing it. Your title suggests that, right?"

"Are you sure you're speaking with the right person?" I asked. "Not sure I understand exactly what you think I can do."

The secretary came in balancing a hot cup of coffee on top of a box of water bottles, which Monty saw out of the corner of his eye. He got up and grabbed the coffee before motioning for the secretary to put the water down on the table by the door.

Opened up the lid to let the steam escape his coffee and kept on going.

"Come on now, you don't need people to tell you what to do. You just go on and do it and say fuck it to whatever is in your way. Okay? That's how we're going to run things now. Kimberly Most is coming in later today, so you two can go over everything. I've got some phone calls to make. Thanks. My door is always open to you—and more to you than to others, but don't tell them that. Okay? Good meeting you, Sarah. You'll do fine. You've been doing fine. You don't need me to tell you anything."

Walked out of his office shaking and trying not to hear the sounds of him gulping down another cup of coffee. Guy must have had wax down his throat to be able to take that much of it in at once.

Kimberly was waiting in the conference room.

"You knew about this?" I mouthed to her.

She shook her head no.

Looked around and saw a bunch of people packing up their things. One of them was Tim, who still hadn't looked me in the eye. Didn't think it was the best idea to let a guy like that go because there was nobody else around here who was going to satisfy Audrey with everything she needed. That woman was the linchpin to a ten-million-dollar account, so somebody was going to have to make her happy. That kind of thing doesn't usually show up on a balance sheet.

Couldn't help but smile until I saw Colin putting a few things into a box.

"What the hell?" I said. "They did you in, too? Hold on for a second, I can probably work it so you stay. Don't worry. Can't believe they'd think about moving on without you!"

"Don't have to do a thing," he said, stopping me from going anywhere. "They actually asked me to stay. Said they'd promote me to creative director if I wanted it. Offered me more. Then more than that even.

"Just that, since I've been here, since I've been sitting in front of these machines, something's gone wrong inside of me. I need to step out. I haven't been able to complete a decent piece in months."

"What are you going to do for money?" I asked, then couldn't believe I asked.

"I need to walk around the city with some cans and markers in my backpack and just be. That's enough for now."

Enough. Hadn't thought about what might be enough. What that final end dollar amount would be that I could save my pops with. How much could I say about the pharmaceutical industry without just playing myself out? How much longer was I going to keep on living the life that others had set out for me?

Started shaking and needed to get out of the office, but couldn't. Everyone was heading into the conference room with Kimberly, and I had to go in there and be briefed when all I really wanted was to just lie there with her and have her comfort me.

There was no time to stop. No moments of transition.

The conference room filled up, and Kimberly started in on her new presentation. She looked at me for a moment, and then purposely didn't for the rest of the time we were in there. Made sense, but didn't feel right. Wasn't interested in making sense anymore. Only wanted to feel something real. Whole.

"We're going to be launching Permafeel," she started. "It helps to slow the night sweats caused by AIDS."

The word AIDS always stopped a room. The myths had all broken down, and now the reality that it was waiting for any-one was right there in your face. This was no BS disease that we needed to create awareness for.

"We're moving into phase two of the clinical trials and have gotten some good results so far. Most of the people we are mar-keting to are IV drug users and prostitutes. We feel that going after homosexuals is going to have negative connotations for those who are not part of that community, so we're going after the addicts and only testing on them.

"The indication is going to be 'for those who have contracted HIV through injections.' This should cover us for blood transfusions as well.

"We've got testing tomorrow, so Sarah, you'll accompany me and report back to the team what we're going to do to target these users. That would be fantastic."

Everyone was taking notes. Wanted to get out of there and hoped that when I did, Kimberly would shed the person she was being in there just like I did. Guess that happens to everyone who works in an office: the person you become when you walk into work has very little to do with you. These people you exist around wouldn't be your friends under normal conditions. You were all drawn together for the money you need to survive. The stories that exist behind all of them—the people they are supporting and lives they need to maintain—have nothing to do with you.

The meeting ended. The day went on. Late. Monty was matching two bottles of water with every cup of coffee and making his way to the bathroom every half hour. Belt slowly cleared away his things and drove off into the distance without saying much more than he already said at the big meeting. He was more of a cog than I'd thought, even though he owned everything. Ownership is temporary.

4.

Before the clinical trials started, I asked the secretary if I could use the phone to try to reach my pops. Hadn't heard his voice for so long. Been too weak to come to the phone, Mom said.

"Hey, Mom," I said. "How is everything?"

"How come you don't once ask me how *I* am," she responded. "I'm the one who needs to deal with all of this! Every day I'm here. I'm alone. You're not alone out there, at least. This isn't fair!"

Heard her pull away from the phone to cry.

"Mom, I'm sorry. That was cold. Sometimes I forget you're there just dealing with it. You're not alone, though. You have Pops with you. Know he's sick and not himself, but he's still there. He's still Pops. Need to talk with him. Need to ask him something."

"He's coming home from the latest round of trials, Sarah. Call tomorrow and he should be up early in the morning. He's always buzzing after what they put inside of him. Usually can't sleep for days."

"Mom."

"Yes, Sarah?"

"You need anything?"

"Your father doesn't want you to come home and see him like this, but I need you to. If you can get away anytime soon, it would help. There's so much we have to go over. I can't do it much longer. I can't."

She hung up the phone. Had to pull myself together to go into testing. Monty was there with coffee and breakfast, sitting like a kid getting ready to watch the circus.

"Send in the clowns!" he said, looking around to see if anyone was laughing at his joke. The people coming in had yet to undergo any testing for the drug. This was more of the crowd we were watching to see how they reacted to various colors, words, and images. They were paid the most, but left behind the greatest side effects.

One by one the junkies came into the viewing room to tell their stories. Some of them were drying out, while others, you could tell, were there to get enough money for their next fix.

"Sarah, do you think we should go with a grungy look for this campaign?" Monty asked. "You know, flannel shirts and Converses. Those are big right now. Even with Kurt Cobain dying, we can still play up on all of that. We should ask these people how many flannel shirts they own. Somebody might want to write down what I'm saying. Can we get some fresh coffee here?"

He poured back the rest of what was in his cup into his mouth and leaned forward to see the next person coming in.

"Do you have a smoke I can bum?" the next subject asked, mumbling a laugh. "Might help me give you what you want to know."

Looked up to match the voice I recognized to the face and saw Kurt sitting there, skinny as ever, if not more so.

"How long have you been infected?" the moderator asked, handing over a cig. "Take your time telling the story."

"I'm not sure how long I've had it," he said, lighting up and sitting back like he was in our old living room. "I just know how long I've known I've had it. Been shooting up for about eight years, so it could have been any of those times. Thanks for the cig, by the way."

"Have you engaged in any homosexual activity?"

He pulled himself together and answered no. Of course, though he was more broken-down than I remember, he knew that this study was only for those who had been infected by needles, so he left the other part of the story out.

Could have stood up there and discredited him, but I didn't care about the integrity of our findings. Nobody really did. We were all doing jobs and did whatever we could to keep them going to support what we needed to support outside of office life. Just going through the proper procedures is all anyone ever cares about.

Thought about how many married men he must have slept with while infected, and how that was spreading AIDS quicker than the needle use. Of course, those married men were not being marched in either, nor were they registered as homosexuals. Still, the spread of an unspoken disease through unspoken-of infidelity was blowing my mind.

Waited for him to finish the interview and leave the room. It was the last one of the day. Needed to get out of there and be alone. Think about what to do next. How I could maneuver in the city that was now closing in around me and taking my thoughts.

Kimberly was too tied up making arrangements for the next round of tests and working out budgets with Monty. Wanted nothing to do with any of it.

Jumped in a cab and had it take me out to the Cliff House. Needed to get away from the machines that were controlling me, so found my way back to the Musée Mécanique. Back to simple machines where you could still feel the human hands that had helped to sculpt. Had to do a double take before letting my brain realize that the shoes sticking out of the Naughty Marietta Cali-O-Scope belonged to Alberto.

He rolled out from underneath with a streak of grease on his chin and smiled at seeing me.

"Thought you were finished with opium dens, laughing clowns, and nudie shows," I said, trying to hide a smile.

Alberto wiped off his hands and walked outside to the ocean with me.

"Picked up a second gig to support the messenger service," he said. "Read about this place in one of your first issues, and it sounded like something I could be a part of. What are you doing out here in the middle of the day?"

"Need to get out, Alberto. It's too much for me now. I've gone far enough inside of this. Was ready to roll a while ago, but now it's become too much."

"If you want out, why don't you leave?"

"Kimberly," I told him, without thinking. "Want to see if I can pull her out with me. Maybe take her back home to Kansas City. We can buy a house out there for pretty cheap and just live. Think I'm ready to just live. Don't want to be a part of anything anymore other than my family."

The barking of seals on the rocks out in the ocean barely reached us. Saw all of those machines ready for Alberto to be working on. Knowing they'd always break down a little made me happy because it meant there would always be a job for him.

"You think Kimberly is going to go with you to Kansas City and live happily ever after?" he asked. "I don't think you realize the kind of person she is. What she's capable of."

"I'm capable of the same type of things," I said. "We all are. No matter where we are in the fight, whatever fight we're engaging in. We're all capable of both sides. Think we've balanced it out, though. Kimberly as well. Without her support, it would have been over for us and there'd be no funding."

"It's in her best interest to see you go on," Alberto said. "She wants to see how far you're going to go. It's part of her study. Can't you see that?"

Wasn't hearing him. Only saw the kitchen table with my pops. Knew he wouldn't care who I brought home as long as we both loved each other. He was the same way as me in that. Done with this city and this industry. Seeing the goat-faced boy on the other side of that glass had shaken me something awful because even though he had stolen my socks and ripped me off, there was no good reason to be testing on him. We knew the drug didn't work.

"Think that's enough," I said. "Can't keep putting out the same story over and over again. Whatever it is that I could have done for this cause, it's done. Time to get out. I'm taking her with me."

"She won't go," he said. "Even if she says she's going to, she can't. She works for something else. She ain't after love."

"You're after love?" I asked him. "I thought you had plans of exposing the truth. Where does love factor into that?"

"That's the very essence of love, Sarah. It doesn't 'factor in.' There's no definite space for it to exist in. Just exists. Lives. Makes its own room."

Vince was calling for Alberto. One of the old nudie-girl machines had broken down again.

Alberto walked into the den of machines, and I was left alone looking over the ocean. He called back out to me again. "I'm going to send you something," he said. "Make sure you're alone when you open it."

Looked over the water and tried to focus on one of the sounds of the seals.

5.

The office was out of control. Cubicles had been built up, and new people were all around. Meetings scheduled every few minutes. The AIDS drug was starting to get some press. Everyone was looking for a cure for that thing, that crazy disease that just broke you down.

Looked over at the desk area where Colin used to be and thought of him in some tunnel somewhere, throwing up a piece and having the time to watch it.

Test results from the interview sessions were on my desk, and just before I was about to pick them up and go through them, a girl swooped them up. She was wearing baggy Freshjive pants and a chain hanging low that I guess connected her wallet to her belt buckle.

"That's totally my bad," she said. "All good, though. I'ma take these, enter all the info in, and send you a link so you can view it all digitally. They told me to do it early this morning, and I thought I'd be able to get to it early, seeing as how most execs don't come in this early. But you beat me here."

Started looking for tickets back home. Went to a website for travel. Got on there and started thinking about Kansas City. Then my mind jumped to the Royals and I wondered how their season was going, so I went onto a sports site to check the standings and saw them in last place. Remembered that when the Royals started losing, I'd switch from the game and put in my mix tapes. Thought about all the music I had on them. Started looking up groups on the site. Then linked off from there onto their new projects. Then to cities they were from. Tours. Places to eat. Recipes. Every few minutes I was on to something next. Left comments in a few places, but that was enough.

A notice popped up in my e-mail box. It was from the intern girl. She'd finished inputting everything. Three hours has passed. Had no idea. Felt hungry after I realized it. Used a new site to find some decent Chinese food, ordered it up without talking to a soul, and started in on the report.

Age. Gender. How the subjects thought they contracted the virus. How long they thought they were going to live. What gave them hope. What their insurance covered. Were their parents still alive. Parents. My pops. Never bought the ticket home. Damn it. Switched back to the website to order the ticket. Was I just getting one ticket, or should I have gotten two and surprised Kimberly? Before I could zero in on a thought, the Internet crashed. IT people were running all over the place. People at their desks had no idea what to do.

Everyone was milling around trying to talk to one another, but all they could talk about was the Internet being down.

Monty put on his jacket and was walking out the door at the same time I was. "You can't sit still either," he said. "Me too. I go for these power walks when I get stifled up. I can think like a bull train when I start going. Want to come with? We'll get some coffee before we go."

Pointed at my platforms and he nodded okay, then made his way out to get a double shot and start his mad march down whatever block could hold him.

Outside. Silence. Walked until I reached North Beach. Middle of the day again, this time without the worry of money or looking for anything. Got a glass of wine from Café Trieste and sat down on the curb outside. The stillness of scattered movement.

Across the street there was an old travel shop with a sign turned around saying, "Be back in 15."

Woman sitting opposite me was on her own curb smoking a cigarette and reading through what was left of the newspaper. She put the butt out under her shoe and took the newspaper in with her to the store. Still holding my wine, I walked across the street and into her world.

"People your age don't come into stores anymore, I heard," she said, pulling the glasses hanging off the end of a piece of yarn up to her eyes. "Where are you looking to go?"

"Home."

She smiled. Could feel her wormhole back to her home. To her Christmas mornings. Her junior high school dance, where she moved close for the first time. They rushed in and out before she found me again.

"Where's that?" she asked.

"Kansas City," I told her. "Missouri."

She moved to her computer and stopped for a minute before figuring out what to do.

"Sorry, honey," she sighed. "My brother convinced me to switch over to this new test program that's supposed to make it easier. It's not easier. Tell you what, why don't you just tell me when you want to go and when you want to come back. When my brother comes in here, I'll let the genius do the extra work."

She pulled a pencil from behind her ear and readied herself at a pad. Realized at that point how rare that combination of movements was becoming.

"Just one-way," I told her. "And let's make the passage for two."

She wrote down the dates I wanted to go and smiled.

"Usually one-way tickets are solo. Nice to see something else might be happening."

"Something else always might be happening," I said. "When can I pick these up?"

She told me she'd be closing at six and I could come by around then if I wanted to.

Back out into the day. Soon I'd be with my pops.

Went to a payphone and called up Kimberly. Noticed the stickers on the side of the booth and the silver ink along the receiver of the phone. Colin was making his rounds and being seen by the people he wanted to see him.

"Can I cook for you tonight?" I said when Kimberly answered.

"Everyone was worried when you just left. Where'd you go?"

"Doesn't matter. Just be there around eight."

Hung up and went shopping for a meal to convince the person I loved to give it all up and jump on a plane with me. Could only do what I knew best. There is a cheese store on Columbus Avenue that sells amazing products, so I bought some gruyere and two fresh mozzarellas, a loaf of bread, and some fresh basil. Butter, I had.

Spent a half hour with the man selling me the cheese, asking him the wine that went best with it. He told me that he saved the cork from the first bottle he ever opened with his wife, and even though she was gone, every time he touched the tip of it, he thought of her face when she smelled it.

Bought the same wine in hopes of having the same memory.

Walked with my bag of groceries back to the ticket spot, picked up my two one-ways to Kansas City, and left the woman arguing with her brother over which method of finding information was best.

6.

Got to my stoop, was about to walk up, and there was Alberto with his messenger bag slung over his shoulder.

"I don't have time for another lecture," I said, trying to move past him. "Big plans tonight. You can pick up the last issue of *Luddite*, but then you have to go."

Opened the door and luckily had the box waiting for him.

Wanted so much to leave the city without telling anyone. Perhaps I could come back someday and drop in on Alberto and his family. Sit down with them all and have a decent cup of coffee after drinking what was waiting for me in Kansas City.

Looked deep at him and saw that he was breaking to tell me something. Was so involved in myself at that point that I thought it was going to be a speech about how he loved me and how I couldn't go. Figured I owed it to the guy to let me know his thoughts before I broke out.

"You look like you're bursting," I said. "You got five minutes before you gotta break because Kimberly's coming over and I need to be fresh when she's here."

"She's playing you," he said. "You'll have to listen now. Not to me. You won't hear what any man other than your father is going to tell you. Here."

He handed me a huge envelope that had been sent from Shaden to an archive center somewhere in New Mexico.

"Assume you opened it," I told him. "You just couldn't wait to catch her in something. You don't think I know what she's done? I've written all about it. What do you think we've been putting out all over the city?"

"Just read it," he said. "And if you leave this city without saying goodbye, just remember this: you and I did something that will exist forever in analog. That's all that matters. All that ever mattered."

He jumped on his bike and rode down Nineteenth Avenue and made a right down Dolores. That's how people exit your life.

Carried the package up the stairs and set it down on the kitchen table next to the groceries. Had the city on me, so I needed to wash it off with a decent shower. Never really had time to wash myself proper. Always running to work or out the door or somewhere. Amazing how much time I'd spend on the insignificant parts of life, but not get the insides of my thighs perfectly clean.

Doorbell rang just as I finished getting dressed. Kim was standing exhausted, her blouse coming out of her jacket and her shoes already off. We kissed in the doorway, and she came in and headed directly for the couch.

The way she just made herself comfortable in my space set me at ease. I'd give her the tickets after dinner.

Sliced both cheeses extremely thin and made sure the cuts of the bread were just right. You know that part in *Love in the Time of Cholera* when he's finally going to sleep with the woman he's been waiting for his whole life? After he had made love to all of those thousands of women just to prepare for this one act of lovemaking?

That's what kind of grilled cheese this was going to be.

Let the butter brown just right. Kimberly lifted up at the smell, but couldn't get off the couch.

"Is it alright if we eat here?" she said. "I might just pass out afterwards. The transition is too much for me right now. Getting to know all of these new players. The budget is up to twenty million. Everyone is going to be paid. Why are they fighting?"

"It's set up that way," I told her. "Groups have to fight against each other or they'll realize how little control they have."

She looked at me a little strange, like she was waiting for me to say something else, but I was too concentrated on the sandwich. Dropped it in and flipped it after a minute and a half. Then let it cook for a minute more.

Perfection.

Opened the bottle of Love Wine and drank myself a decent glass.

Finished, I walked over to the couch and put the wine and sandwiches on the coffee table. She sat up and grabbed a half with one hand and a glass with the other. She kissed me in the middle.

Could tell by her face that it was one of the best things she ever ate. She matched each bite with a sip of wine.

"I want you to move with me back to Kansas City," I told her. "Just so we can recover. We can move on from there, but I need to touch home for a bit. Want to do it with you."

She took another bite and kept her eyes on me before they closed.

"Sarah, my life is here. I don't need to move on from anything. I've built what I wanted here. This is what I was meant to do. I thought you wanted to be part of that."

She yawned and was slipping out of the moment.

"You knew I was doing everything I could to destroy that," I told her. "You were helping me. I don't understand. Why would you want to stay inside when you know how rotten it is?"

She laughed with her last bit of energy.

"There's nothing coming down, love," she said, doing a final stretch. "There's too much behind it. The reach is spectacular. What you did, what you're doing, I love it. It makes me love you. But really, there was no way you could win. There is no victory. Kansas City, that's cute. Cute. You're cute. I need cute in my life."

She passed out without finishing her sandwich.

Knew she was exhausted, but still, she just blew me off.

Looked over at the table and realized that Alberto's package was still sitting there unopened. Made my way over with my grilled cheese, the rest of Kimberly's, and the bottle.

Took a good sip, then another, and opened it up.

As soon as I started reading it, I knew what it was. Amazing. She was lying right on my couch. Thought she was different and that she shared the same thing inside that Alberto and I had. But this is what he had been telling me about her all along.

All the time I'd thought we had been the ones studying others. In front of me was a report on the effects of working in an environment where people communicate using computers for more than six hours a day. How it affects their ability to reason, as well as to communicate with each other.

Each page had a different PopCore employee's picture on it, along with the time they spent on individual websites, what sites they visited, how long they stayed on each, and if they did the work they were assigned.

It was all graphed out. We were each assigned personality types.

Colin's was "street artist." Bad upbringing. Parents not around much growing up. Into graffiti and hip-hop. Draws constantly. They even had overhead shots of what he was drawing in his notebooks. Cameras above. They had been monitoring everything.

We were the actual case study.

My profile had it all. Things I had said on my interview. How I dealt with different situations. Every e-mail I had written. The words I repeated more than three times. Even the things about my father that I had told Kimberly in bed. It was all there, including the way I interpreted the information in the zines. It was all being used and studied.

My last piece of solid ground in the double life I was living shook beneath me.

It was all on the effects of running an office dominated by computers and e-mails. It was us who had developed ADD. All of this was being sent to the research facility so that the doctors there could write their papers and then get the disease approved.

It was amazing. Fascinating.

The studies said that employees sitting in front of a computer with access to the Internet are ten times more likely to develop ADD than those without Internet access. Of course, it also stated that it was the Internet itself that was causing the ADD. If the drug companies hadn't actually created the Internet to inflict ADD on people, they'd certainly helped spread the infection. And who was to say they hadn't created it? The Internet, this magnificent beast that was eroding SF at its core, was probably no more than a case study by the pharmaceutical companies to start a global ADD epidemic.

Kimberly had been studying it all. We were the rats.

Saw her asleep on my couch, and I had crazy thoughts running through my head. The first being to just set a torch to the whole place and let her go up with it, but you can't just go and do something like that. Seen too many movies that have you getting caught and just spending your life in jail. Not me. Had to get back to my pops.

Looked around at what to take with me and there was nothing, really. Hadn't bought anything since I'd been in San Francisco.

Then I saw a stack of *Luddite*s in a corner. I took one of each issue, wrapped them in duct tape, tossed them in my bag, and headed to the door. Before I walked out, I went into her purse and took all her cash. Nearly five hundred bucks she had in there. Had her paycheck as well—ten grand. That was for two weeks. Don't think it wasn't. Took that as well, along with her wallet. We looked pretty much the same at that point, so going to a check cashing spot down on Market Street, one that took a nice percentage for doing those things, wouldn't be a problem.

Didn't even look back as I headed out the door. Had my plane ticket, the zines I had worked my ass off on.

Home.

Jumped in a cab and had him wait outside the check cashing spot for me. Was an easy one. Back in and out towards Market Street. Asked him if he wouldn't mind taking one last lap around the city, and passed all the spots I had spent my last three years in. When I reflected on the life I'd lived in San Francisco, I didn't want any people in those images, just the places and my own thoughts inside of them.

And so we went, through the streets before the analog age caved in and was replaced by a digital world meant to drug you out. Checked my watch. Didn't want to miss my plane, so we headed out and onto the freeway, away from the city for the last time and towards the airport.

I was coming, Pop.

CHAPTER 18

i.

Back in Kansas City in the winter. Cold is something you don't experience in the Bay Area. It gets foggy and wet and can creep up on you, but the cold doesn't go through you like it does here.

Remember being in the airport and how empty it was. Mom wasn't there to pick me up, probably because she was getting Pops ready to see me.

The emptiness of the airport back home was no doubt the subtraction of San Francisco in my life.

Into a cab and through the wet streets of Kansas City. Even though it was cold, I kept a window rolled down so I could hear a train whistle if it happened to blow. Didn't want to miss that. Been waiting for years to hear that. Not sure what I was going to do or how long I was going to stay out here, but at least until I felt at home.

The longer I was out of the office, the more I felt like myself. Something happens in those cubicles that you can't help. It all just seeps into you, and you find yourself becoming something that you are not. Now I knew the reason: They create situations and study how you act in them. You are the test audience.

The closer to the house we got, the better I felt. Was going to see my pops for the first time in years. Had brought the fixings for the grilled cheese home with me—it was for him, anyway. Guess throughout my time in San Francisco I was always looking for someone to satisfy. Sending money home is okay, but you can't see the reaction. Can't feel the connection.

Through those old streets that held old ghosts. Kids sat on steps and smoked just far enough from the window so that it wouldn't go inside and get to their parents.

Pulled up to my house, paid the driver, and saw my mom waiting for me on the front porch. She didn't let me take two steps before she flew towards me and wrapped both arms around me and squeezed harder than she ever had. Tried to hug her back, but it was like she was preventing me from moving. Finally, slowly, she let go.

"Where's all your things, Sarah?" she asked, wiping the tears off her face. "Figured you'd have stacks of things you'd be bringing home."

"Only thing I wanted to bring home was myself," I told her. "And this amazing cheese for Pops. Been dreaming about making him one. He's in the house?"

Took a few steps to the house and looked back to my side to say something to my mom, but she wasn't there. Stood in the same place she'd hugged me.

"Come on, Mom, I'll make you one too."

"Sarah…"

"What is it, Mom?"

"Sarah."

Ran into the house to find my pops. Yelled everywhere. Went into every room. Upstairs. To the basement. Backyard. Into the kitchen, where I saw my mom sitting at the table with a checkbook under her hands.

"Come and sit, Sarah."

"I don't want to sit! Where is he? At the hospital again?"

She looked out the window and didn't break her stare until the faint noise of the train whistle moved her back to the moment.

"Sit down," she said, rubbing her hands over a checkbook. "Do you want to make a grilled cheese?"

Sat down at the table without saying a word. My mom knew me well enough to know it was time to tell me what she'd been holding back.

"Sarah, dear," she started, "he hasn't been with us for some time. Now, you have to understand, he wanted it this way. You know your father—you know when he set his mind to things being done as he wanted them. There was no stopping that.

"He passed almost a year ago. After you started working and making money. Real money. He didn't want you to watch it all, and he didn't want any part of those clinical trials. He knew they were all phony and designed to make money for the drug companies. Once he knew you were working for them and writing about them, he realized that you'd be able to expose that."

"Why wouldn't you tell me then? All those times I called and wanted to speak with him. He was gone then?"

"Yes."

"How could you have done that? Could have come home years ago! All that money I sent home—it was supposed to be for him. Where did it go?" Looked around and saw that not one thing had changed from when I'd grown up, so it wasn't like she'd been taking the money herself. "What did you do with it?"

She pushed the bank book over to me. Inside there was a letter from my pops. Opened it up and looked over at my mom, who was silently bawling her eyes out. Felt the deepness of her gasping inhales inside my chest.

Dear Sarah,

Please take a moment to understand. You couldn't do anything, and I didn't want them experimenting on me. We both feel the same way about those people. The money you sent home, most of it, has been saved in a bank account for you. By the time you come home, it should be enough so that you can do whatever you like without having to answer to anyone else.

You went out there to save me, and now I want you to save yourself. Take what you have learned and put it out into the world. You can use this to make whatever you like and, more importantly, get the truth out there. You are my little creator and my best girl.

It is my gift to you, to give you back what you wanted to give to me. I will be inside you forever, and exist in whatever you decide to put into the world. Don't be angry at your mother, it was my dying wish. Now we're both free. You've allowed me to do something amazing with my life—I made you.

Be what you wish with your freedom.

Love,

Pops

Bawling, I looked up at my mother, who had taken the fixings for the grilled cheese and started making us something. She kept the lie going for him because he wanted my reality that was now possible to be his truth. Was glad he never participated in any of those trials.

"I'm not anywhere near the chef you are, Sarah," she said, sucking in her tears, "but I'll try."

Jumped up and hugged her from behind. It was the most in love with my mother that I had ever been. The two of us realized right there that we were all that we had left in the world.

Collapsed back to the table and looked at the checkbook. Said there was around two hundred and fifty grand inside. The smell of the grilled cheese shot through me. We sat down and ate slowly, both of us wishing that my pops might have tasted one of the bites.

After we finished in silence, my mother brushed away her tears.

"What did you bring home with you?" she said. "What's in the bag?"

Pulled out the issues of *Luddite* duct taped together and put them in the middle of the table.

"Must be valuable," she said.

"I guess they are," I told her—and, I guess, myself as well. "If they got out to enough people, they just might be."

Think that was the first moment my mother and I knew exactly what the other was thinking. Could feel my pops as well at the table with us, his hands on the duct-taped issues of the past three years of my life.

I could hear his voice:

"Sarah, you can show your work to the world now. They need to know."

Now you do.

The End

ACKNOWLEDGMENTS

To the city of San Francisco—forever my home, my center, and the start of anything real that grew inside of me.

To Erika Fazio, who kept pestering me to write this damn book already. Here it is, Erika—happy now?

To Terry Goodman—you take every call and are the one who believed from the jump. Thanks for bringing Sarah Striker out to the world and being such a champion.

To David Downing—Thanks for using the knife to carve instead of cut.

To Nikki Sprinkle—Welcome aboard this crazy ride. I can feel your energy spreading throughout the universe.

To Jacque Ben-Zekry—You sent dolphins and cookies when we needed them most. Amazing heart you have.

To Sarah Tomashek—despite my insanity, you always keep it cool and make sure the right eyes are falling on the work. Props.

To Noah Amine, who was there when I was just scribbling notes and trying to find a way to get the story out there. Only you know the true roots of *Pharmacology* madness.

To Kerrie Robertson and Blair Mastantuno, for making sure the cover was just right and dealing with my madness.

To Jessica Smith, for running this book through the car wash and making it ready for its first ride out to the world.

To my amazing wife Saruul, who dealt with the sleepless nights and wandering mind while I was giving birth to this story. Without you, existence would only be the days on the calendar. With you, it's a life. Everything is for you.

ABOUT THE AUTHOR

From selling his books on the streets of New York City, to having his first novel, *The Last Block in Harlem*, published and read across the globe, Christopher Herz has not taken the traditional literary route. His follow-up novel, *Pharmacology*, continues in his tradition of taking readers into a reality they don't want to believe, but cannot turn themselves away from. Christopher lives with his wife in Brooklyn and is constantly working towards his mission of connecting the people of the world through literature.